■ ■ ■

THE AFTERMATH

From a long distance away the bodies beside the road looked like piles of stones. They were the new dead. One face showed at the edge of the heap. All the hair was gone, even the eyebrows. The face was heavy, a broad nose and a heavy chin, and ears that seemed to be too big. The eyes were closed behind red, puffy lids, and I wondered what color they had been.

Then I saw the soft, pink collar where it rested against the throat, and the flower-shaped cluster of pearls. It was a woman, changed even more than the others, not a woman anymore. Not a man. Something else....

■ ■ ■

NEENA GATHERING

NEENA GATHERING

VALERIE NIEMAN COLANDER

PAGEANT BOOKS

PAGEANT BOOKS
225 Park Avenue South
New York, New York 10003

Copyright © 1988 by Valerie Nieman Colander

**PAGEANT and colophon are trademarks
of the publisher**

Cover artwork by Keith Parkinson

Printed in the U.S.A.

First Pageant Books printing: July, 1988

10 9 8 7 6 5 4 3 2 1

*To Fred Chappell, who saw promise
in Neena when she was young.*

To my family for their support

And always, and always, to John.

Inter canem et lupum

NEENA GATHERING

PART I

Chapter One

———◆———

IT WAS EARLY in the year. The sap was up in the
trees, and at the ends of the branches the buds
showed red and green against the pale sky.
There was a light breeze from the south, making
the branches tremble and sway as though the
new life was moving them.

We were up near the top of the ridge, where
there had at one time been a cleared field. Now
it was overgrown with wild cherry trees, young
ones, seeded from the forest into the abandoned
field. Their bark was smooth and dark red, the
color of the mahogany chest where Aunt Maura
stores the clothes out of season, layered in with
lavender and sweet fern to keep away mold and
moths.

This was the best time to gather cherry bark,

when the sap ran in the trees and the bark would peel off in whole sheets, including the thin inner bark which was used for a tonic and in cough remedy. When my friend Ditsky-the-Peddler came by on what he called his "spring mud route," we would have bundles of this inner bark, peeled and dried, waiting to trade.

Aunt Maura stood by a group of pole-sized trees, her cloth-lined collecting basket in her hand. She looked at the trees in that way she has of sizing things up, people or things. Her round face was red from the climb to the top of the ridge and she had opened up her plaid jacket. She shook the old cockleburs from her pant legs, breathed out once, loudly, then set the basket down.

I took another stand a little way away. The trees grew in a circle around a gray stone, which shouldered up through last year's dead grass. Between their branches I could see, to the south, the fallen-in roof of the old Kisner place and the faint line of the overgrown road.

I took the knife and made two cuts around the tree, one right under the first branches and another a handspan below. The knife slid sideways once, around a cankered place. There was a sudden clean smell, the ooze of tree juice through the bark that smelled like spring.

With the releasing cut between the circles, the outer bark came off nicely, peeling away from the light green underbark and curling back into circles as I threw it down. When I first came to her, Aunt Maura had brought back these rounds of bark for me to play with. She sewed the bark together and made a cradle, but I cried because I didn't have a doll to put in it. She took the cradle and threw it on the kindling pile. When she put it in the stove I cried again.

I began to peel away the inner bark. It was moist with the rising sap and came away from the white wood easily. The sun made the wood shine like snow.

"You're doing good, Neena, but try to take the bark off in wider strips if you can."

I looked over to where Aunt Maura was working. She was on her second tree already, the first one standing naked from knee height to the middle, where the first large branches stretched out and up, hoping for the sun and not knowing yet that they'd been cut off from the root-life.

Cherry bark gathering was easy, just find a stand of young trees and cut them. It was a lot easier than finding goldenseal or motherwort, though I could find those, too. Aunt Maura said I had a talent as an herbalist, if I'd develop the patience.

"It's too early for hepatica, yet?"

She looked back at me, her brown eyes seeing sharp, and nodded. "It's just pushing through the ground now. What else comes early?"

"Skunk cabbage, bloodroot and twinleaf. Coltsfoot."

"Don't forget shepherd's purse."

Aunt Maura took a lot of time in trying to teach me about herbs and roots, though I was slow sometimes to remember. I didn't even know what shepherd's purse was when I came to her, much less that it was good for treating scurvy and for making urine come. Now when I walked through the woods or by the stream, I could name most of the plants, knowing which ones were good for what illnesses. This made my eighth year with Aunt Maura, and for seven of those years I'd helped collect.

The woods were starting to liven up from the sun and the south wind. Snow was gone everywhere, even in the north shadows of the slopes. Chickweed, which was green under the snow all winter, was showing little white blossoms. Even the mosses on the gray boulder looked brighter.

I moved to the next tree. It was crooked in the middle. I made the two trunk-circling cuts, then began to slice down, following the curve in the trunk. The knife point sank in too deep; I could feel it biting into the wood. I pulled it out and began again, kneeling and resting my hand against the trunk so I could guide the knife better.

Suddenly, a hawk cried overhead. At the same time I felt the knife slip, and felt the cold numbness of a cut on my thumb. I pulled my hand back, the blood running. Looking up, I saw the hawk slipping away from the height of the ridge, its wings balanced on the wind.

I don't remember saying anything, but Aunt Maura was there. She pulled out the tail of her shirt and pressed it against the cut.

"So much for haste," she said.

I blushed, knowing that she knew I had hurried, trying to keep up with her.

The blood soaked through the brown cloth and made a dark stain. I watched it spread.

I fell down when the explosion came. There was a sound like a book falling—whump, but much louder—and the ground shook and the air was still and then it rushed by us. I remember my knee bleeding from hitting the concrete. Glass broke and fell, tinkling. Stones fell from all the buildings —square blocks, and panels which broke like glass, and fancy pieces. A piece like the tail of a fish, curved and scaled, fell right in front of us. Then we ran downstairs into the basement of a building, where there was a dark room. There were other people in the room. One of them was moaning.

Mom held my hand and we walked toward the back of the room. People pushed against us, but not because they were angry. They were just there, like us, frightened. We sat down next to the wall, behind a table. There were glasses on the table.

"I'm thirsty," I said.

"Hsssh, Daneen."

"Where are we?"

"This is a safe place."

"Where?"

"It's a tavern—a place where people come to be together."

"We're together now."

And somebody laughed next to us in the darkness, a voice between a woman's and a man's.

"Who did it?" said the person who laughed. I

tried to look over Mom's lap, but all I could see was a shadow.

"The goddamned Lakes Autonomy, that's who. Motherfuckers." It was a deep, angry voice, from the center of the room.

"Please, there's a little girl here," the shadow person said.

"There's worse things than words," he growled, but he didn't say anything else.

"Why do you say it was the Lakes Autonomy?" Mommy said, staring out toward the center of the room.

"My brother's in the City Guard. He said they've been watching for this."

"Then why did the planes get through?" A woman's voice. She sounded nice. Tired, but nice.

"There was only one explosion. Maybe only one got through."

The shaking came up through the carpet on the floor.

"Two."

There were a lot of little noises in the room. They made a sound all together like cars on the street in the rain. I could hear the moaning, very soft, and somebody sniffling. A tinkle of glass, and I thought that glass was falling and breaking in here, too, but then there was a pop and a hissing sound, and the sound of someone drinking. I wanted something to drink again.

"But why?" Mom said. It frightened me to hear her voice shaking, too, like the others. "Why are we doing this to each other?"

"Too many people, too many differences," said the shadow person. "Too many people, and not

*enough things—not like there was. Not enough,
and no one thinks he's getting his share. New England is cold and the Lakes Autonomy is hungry.
Sutherland feels threatened . . ."*

*"And here in the Coastal Cities we think we can
tell everyone else what to do because of a few
damn monuments in Washington," said the deep
voice.*

*"What do you think," said a new voice, "was in
the bomb?"*

Everyone was very quiet.

"Metachemicals?"

"No—no way."

*"I heard that metachemicals were used on
Akron last week."*

"Where'd'ya hear that?"

"A broadcast."

"Out of the Lakes Autonomy, I suppose."

*"This was just a bomb," said the deep-voiced
man over the tangle of voices. "Explosives. A bomb
to knock down buildings and scare us."*

Mom hugged me. I heard more bottles opening.

"Neena."

"Yes."

"The bleeding's stopped."

It was Aunt Maura, not my own mother. She
took the cloth away. The cut ran from the
knuckle into the fat part below the thumb on
my left hand, a gash that opened and showed
red flesh when I flexed my thumb a little.

"Here." She tore a strip of cloth from her shirt

and took my hand. She wrapped the cloth around and tied it, to keep the wound closed.

"You just don't have patience, Neena. With knives, or anything. Lord knows in the garden you're as quick to pull up carrots as weeds."

"I'm sorry."

Aunt Maura looked at me for a moment, then set my hand down carefully in my lap and went back to her collecting.

I couldn't do much now but trim stray bits of outer bark away from the thin, inner strips. I used the point of my knife to lift them away, then laid the bark on the clean cloth that lined the collecting basket.

Aunt Maura worked quickly and cleanly. Cut, peel, strip, and move to the next tree. She was a big woman, and her hands were thick with work, dark in the creases from working with the roots and barks. Even so, she seemed to do everything well, whether it was something delicate like sorting seeds and mending clothes, or rougher work like splitting wood and raking hay. She could lay a fire in the kitchen stove that would last right through the night and leave starting embers for morning.

Her brown hair was streaked with gray, regular streaks like furrows, and was gathered back to be tied by a piece of shoelace. My mother's hair was red, like mine, and she didn't wear dark clothes but ones which were bright green and blue, and soft to the touch. I remembered the silky feel of them, like water across my fingers.

After I first came across the mountains with

Ditsky-the-Peddler, it seemed as if I spent every day waiting for Mom to come after me and take me back with her, to Baltimore where we lived in a brick house with a big lawn. I used to look out the door just before I went to bed, every night, to make sure that she wasn't coming down the path that I had come down.

Now I knew that the cities were all gone. I knew that most of the people were gone, too, the children that I had played with, and the woman in the red smock at the All-Nite Store, and the man who mowed our lawn. All dead. If she had intended to come after me, she never made it.

Thinking about it made my chest tight from wanting to cry.

"Last spring, Ditsky wanted as much prickly ash, mullein and cranesbill as we could gather," Aunt Maura said. "Cholera, dysentery and typhoid. They'll be back this summer, I imagine. But this being spring, he'll want things for pneumonia and scurvy, and tonics, of course." She paused. "Neena?"

"Yes." It took all my breath.

"What's the best for lung problems?"

"Lobelia herb, true spikenard." I thought for a moment. "And bloodroot and pleurisy root."

"We've still got pleurisy root in the storeroom. I imagine it'll fetch a good price."

She brought over a bundle of bark and set it in the basket. "No need to check it, it's clean," she said.

The afternoon went away while Aunt Maura stripped every tree of its bark. The field looked like a field of ghost trees, thin and white. They were ghost trees because they would all die now that their bark was gone. But other trees would come here.

The cold started to set in. The sun was low in the sky, red through the trees. Aunt Maura buttoned up her coat, and we started back.

Near the little falls on the stream that runs down to the river, we spooked a doe deer, her belly heavy with the fawns she would have in June. She ran, crashing through the brush, and her tail could be seen white among the trees for a long time.

From the edge of our meadow, the house was a square, black shadow, surrounded by the branchwork of maple trees. The barn was a low black hump to the left. We stood there for a long time, watching and listening, until the sun was down and there was just enough light left in the sky to see our way clear among the dead hummocks of grass and the standing clumps of old weeds.

The stars were coming out. There was a star where the sun had just disappeared. And there was a dark cloud rising from the land, across the stars.

I breathed in. I could smell the cow-odor of Heidi and Sunny in their stalls, and beyond that a sweet burning of clean wood, not the bad smell of trash or the choking smell of a barn burning, full of hay.

Aunt Maura sniffed and looked at the smoke rising. "The barterman must be clearing brush," she said.

We stamped the dirt from our feet on the stone by the entryway and went inside. There was a rosy glow of a banked fire behind the mica-glass of the stove, and the warmth spread from there into my bones.

Chapter Two

———◆———

"GO INTO THE house and get the Winchester."

Aunt Maura kept looking at the ground, and she spoke in a low, plain voice.

"Don't look around. Just go to the house. Then watch."

I threw the rock in my hand to the side of the garden and walked toward the house. My back tingled, as if my spine and skin could see the threat that Aunt Maura had seen.

I went up the stone walk and opened the door, went in, and shut it carefully behind me. Then I ran quietly to the front room where the rifle rested above the big chair, took it down, and checked to make sure it was loaded.

How many people were there? A band of raiders? Three, a dozen? I opened the drawer in the little marble-topped table and took six more bullets from the box.

The kitchen window looked out over the garden

and part of the path that came up from the road to Middletown. Slowly, I went up to the window.

Everything looked flat and gray under the overcast sky. Aunt Maura was a brown hump on the bare ground of the garden. The trees, which just the other day had been glossy with new buds, were gray, lifeless. The cows stood under the barn eaves with their heads hanging.

There was a little jump of movement far down the path, where it curved up from what we still called the hard road, though it was mostly broken and heaved and half-covered with growth. The movement was a single person, a man leaning forward as he slowly worked his way up the slope. All that you could tell about him was that he had light hair.

I clicked off the safety and rested the barrel on the window ledge. It was worn gray, the color of the sky.

Aunt Maura kept working, throwing stones and trash out of the garden. She didn't look up or any way show that she knew there was a stranger on the path.

The light-haired man might just be someone after herbs to cure a baby's croup. He might also be some wanderer looking to take what he could.

The man came closer. He looked to be tall and very lean. He wore a blue shirt that was too big for him, and sand-colored pants. He carried a small pack, which showed that he was a traveler, but not any gun or knife that could be seen. That all by itself didn't seem right because there wasn't a person who went off without some kind of weapon, openly seen, if he were on the road now.

He stopped and stared up at the house, then out across the meadow and the sag-roofed barn, as if he were trying to remember something. He looked at Aunt Maura kneeling in the garden.

"Is this the Daucherty place?" he called, his voice raspy.

Aunt Maura didn't say anything.

"I'm looking for Maura Daucherty."

"And who are you?" she called back, still staying low.

"Ted Daucherty."

"Ted!" She looked up. "Ted!" She sprang up and ran through the garden, loose clods of earth kicking up behind her. She ran down the steep hill by the garden, her arms flying up and down to keep her balance, and into the path.

The man—her brother Ted, my own uncle— walked toward her. He moved like he was tired right down to his bones.

I put the safety back on, and went and laid the Winchester back on its rests in the front room. Then I went outside and stood by the corner of the house, waiting for them to come up.

Ted Daucherty leaned on Aunt Maura's shoulder as they came up the path, his head down. His blond hair was long and hung loose over his shoulders, and he had a thick, red beard that hid his mouth and chin.

"The only thing I had to go by was your letters," he was saying. "When you moved up here, five, six years before the wars started."

Aunt Maura's expression wavered between

happiness and surprise. "I knew then that things were going to hell," she said, and her voice, like her face, was strange and excited.

"The letters, what I could remember, said you lived near what used to be called Middletown, in an old farmhouse on Laban's Ridge. This place seemed to match as soon as I saw it."

He lifted his head, and I couldn't help but gasp. His eyes were bright blue, the same color as my mother's, and my own. The set of them under eyebrows arched like bird wings, even the straight line of his nose—his face was my mother's face, the way I remembered it. The only thing about him that resembled Aunt Maura were the lines of worry and fatigue around his mouth, half-hidden by the beard. But his blue eyes darted, moving like a wary animal's, and his forehead was scarred from the part of his hair to his brow, a deep, ugly gash that was only recently healed.

"Terra—" he said, and his voice was full with wonder.

"This is Daneen. Terra's child."

"Of course. I saw a picture of you, in your cradle," he said, then he stepped forward and put his hands on my shoulders. "You were bald as an egg, then."

He squeezed my shoulders.

"You're quite a girl now. You've got your mother's eyes," and he paused, as if he'd lost the way of his thought, "and her hair."

I wanted to tell him that when I looked at him I could see my mother, just like he saw her in me, but instead I blurted, "Have you seen her, my Mom, in the city?"

He seemed to sag a little. "No. I haven't seen her."

We were all quiet for a minute.

"Well, let's go in and sit down. You've had a long walk, brother."

We went in and sat at the round kitchen table. There were four ladder-back chairs—had always been four—but now, with just the one empty, it made me think of my Mom and where she might be.

"Would you like coffee, Ted?" Aunt Maura asked.

He smiled for the first time, showing beautiful white teeth. "You live well here."

"It's not coffee, really. Dandelion and chicory root, roasted."

"And do you have tea as well?"

"Just the kinds that are good for what ails you, herbals. And I'm afraid we won't have any milk until the cow freshens."

"But we've got good cider," I said. "We went halves with the Hollises and pressed with their press, and we each got a barrel."

"If Daneen says it's good, I'll go with that," he said, smiling again. "If you've got enough."

"Neena, run to the springhouse and bring in a jar. And bring a piece of that cheese."

I ran, and I didn't even stay in the springhouse to watch the water flow through the moss.

When I got back, the table was spread with bread and pickles and a wrinkled piece of sausage that was going to be for our dinner. I put down the cider and cheese, and Ted leaned back in his chair, just looking at the food.

"I haven't seen food like this since—who knows when," he said, beginning to load up his plate. He cut the whole end off the loaf of bread and took a big chunk of sausage.

I sat down in the chair next to his. The bullets in my shirt pocket jingled.

"Don't tell my you've got silver and gold in your pocket," he said, teasing.

"No."

"Jewels?"

"Just bullets." I took them out of my pocket and went to the little table, put them back in the box.

Ted was looking at Aunt Maura.

"We didn't know who was coming up the path," she explained. "I set Neena to watch. With the Winchester."

He swallowed a big bite of cheese and washed it down with cider. "Bad here, too?"

"Bad enough," said Aunt Maura. "It's not safe to live alone, and it's not safe to live together. Middletown's been burned three times and raided I don't know how many, until just a few hang on there."

"Soldiers?"

"Some of them are soldiers, or ex-soldiers, and others are just people from the cities. They'll take food or what have you. Some of the raiders will kill just as easy as look at you, if you give them a reason. And then there are the Harvesters over in Penitence, though they've never bothered us."

"Harvesters? Penitence?"

"It's a religion. They call themselves the Lord's Harvest People. They've got five or six other walled villages; Penitence is the closest. They believe they're the chosen people, and that they have to remain faithful while the world goes through the Great Tribulation before they're taken up to heaven."

"There are a lot of those kind around. Milleni-alists."

"The Harvesters are a little different," she said. "They also believe that sinners can be saved—but that they have to die immediately or they'll fall back into sin. So they've been known to take people off the roads and farms to 'save' them. Then they kill them and send them to heaven."

He stared at her. "That's a new wrinkle."

"I would imagine you'd have seen about everything. Were you still in Norfolk when all this hit? Working for that chemical company?"

"I was caught there when the Sutherland declared its independence. Washington sent troops against the city, and to Charleston and Atlanta, but they were wiped out—the Sutherland held the chemweapons stores, and enough aircraft and weaponry from the federal bases to take out a hundred armies."

"Or a hundred cities," Aunt Maura said softly. "We didn't hear much up here but rumors after New England split away."

"That's when everything unraveled. There's a new English Canada, which took over most of upstate New York, with the governor's approval.

The Lakes Autonomy was declared at Pontiac. Everything else between here and the Japanese coast is just a patchwork of bare ground and little ragged kingdoms, except for Texas. At least that's what I've heard."

"The cities are dead. The power network is gone, the communications are gone. When the lights went, everything went," she said. "Ted, I don't think you could populate greater Washington with all the people left east of the Mississippi and north of Tennessee."

"Is there any authority here?"

"We get a truck from the Pittsburgh Hierarchy through the area about once a year, out on the big road. I don't know what they're after."

He snorted. "Laying claim, or trying to. The Pittsburgh Hierarchy is a few dozen families out past Monessen. They were a survivalist camp, so they've got guns and fuel stashed. They're trying to claim most of northern West Virginia as their territory, but they don't own it any more than the Sutherland does. The Appalachians are pretty much no-man's-land."

"It sounds like you know a lot about the wars."

"Enough," he said, and cleared his throat.

"Why did you wait so long to leave? And how did you make it to here?"

I stopped chewing on a crust of bread to listen. If he could make it here after this long, maybe my mother could, too.

"It's a long story. A bay fisherman I knew took me out of Norfolk to the Delaware side, and I stayed with a fishing family there," he said, looking down at his plate and sorting a seed away from the pickle. "Then, after most of the bombing and fighting was done in that area, I came across the mountains by way of the old Maryland corridor. But Daneen—how did she come to be here?"

"They were living outside of Hagerstown when the cholera started," said Aunt Maura quietly. "Terra put her in care of a peddler who comes through this area."

She put her hand up and brushed back his hair, touched the edge of the wound on his forehead. "How did this happen?"

He pulled his head away from her touch. "A run-in—I'd rather not talk about it," he said. "So, it's just you and me left, Maura Lee."

"People sometimes take a long time to get back. Look how long it took you," she said, and I knew it was mostly for me, because she knew I still hoped, and not because she had any hope.

"Tell me how you live here," he said.

"We have a yoke of oxen. The cow, Heidi, will drop a calf next month, courtesy of Smith's bull. She's a Brown Swiss, and Sunny, the steer, is some mixed breed, but he works all right with her as the lead. We keep a big garden."

"What do you do for goods? Cloth, ammunition, the like?"

"We collect medicinals in the woods, plants and roots and barks. Most of the land has grown back. We dry them and some we trade for pack goods from Ditsky-the-Peddler—he's the one that brought Neena here—and the really valuable, rare ones I take to the barterman."

"Who?"

Aunt Maura motioned to the west.

"He's our closest neighbor, a couple of miles overland. I couldn't tell you where he came from, exactly, except it was from the cities. He's taken the name Arden. He's been Changed."

Ted jumped as though something had bit him. "Are you sure?"

"Lord, yes, Ted. He's lost every bit of his hair, and his skin is this funny yellow color. And his face and hands are heavy-like—the bones and flesh are grown over. You've seen what the metachemicals do. He came here and built a log cabin, back in a grove of pines all by himself, and then soon enough we learned that he had connections with the city scavengers and that he'd take barter. I don't know what we'd do for things like kerosene and ammunition if it wasn't for the barterman."

"I didn't think too many survived," he said. It seemed to bother him that we lived close to the barterman. I never yet had seen him, even so.

"I can't think of seeing another Change anywhere around. They say there was a woman Change leading a band of raiders, but then truth turns to tales as it goes along."

He poured himself another glass of cider and drank it down, the bubbles curling in his mustache. He wiped away the foam and set the glass back down on the table.

"Are you going to stay, Ted?"

"Uncle Ted," said Aunt Maura.

"Uncle Ted."

He leaned back in his chair and looked at me, solemn, then smiling, with his blue eyes crinkling at the corners.

"I suppose that's why I came," he said.

Chapter Three

———◆———

THE BUTTERFLY WAS a month early, and it flew slowly from the tip of one dry grass-stem to another. It was a cabbage butterfly, white. Sometimes you'd see them or the sulphur butterflies even in mid-January, if there came sunny weather and a long thaw.

It rested on a dandelion flower, opening and closing its wings in the sun.

All the noise and activity didn't seem to bother it—harness chains rattling, the cows stamping, the calf bawling in the barn with its nose pressed against the gate that kept it separated from its mother. It was a fine day after a dry week, and we were going to break new ground.

The calf bawled again. Heidi mooed once, her head stretched out at the end of her neck and her brown eyes closed, but she stayed. Aunt Maura led up Sunny. Uncle Ted set the poplar yoke over their necks and fastened the chains to the iron steeple-ring that hung down from the center.

"Wouldn't this be easier with a horse?" he said.

"Not unless you want to shoe it, and cut and stack extra hay to feed it, and doctor it when it comes up lame twice a year," she answered. "Oxen can plow and haul a wagon, and they're tough. Heidi gives us milk and a calf every year, and when these two are past working, we'll have beef and hides."

"All right!" Uncle Ted backed away with his hands in the air. Aunt Maura smiled.

"Besides," she said, serious, "I can't afford to get a horse and harness. I'd have to barter away one awful lot of herbs."

"That won't be a problem after this fall," he said.

"Maybe."

"I guarantee it."

Uncle Ted, in long evening talks sitting by the stove, had persuaded Aunt Maura to open up some new ground and plant it to corn. He said that he could rig a distillery unit and make liquor.

Aunt Maura didn't seem to be so sure, though I couldn't tell if she doubted he could make good liquor, or whether she was concerned about the extra work. One thing, liquor should be worth a lot in barter. More even than lady-slipper root, hard as that was to find.

"Come on, Neena, quit dawdling," she called.

I got up, and the butterfly lifted itself from the flower and flew slowly away.

Heidi shook herself, making the wood and metal rattle, settling her bones against the yoke. Aunt Maura stepped behind the plow and put her hands on the long wooden handles. I went up and took Heidi's halter to help lead the team straight.

Uncle Ted, because he wasn't used to handling the oxen, followed behind the plow to pick up stones and roots.

The ground was hard as a board, packed, the same heavy yellow clay that made the garden sticky after wet weather and cracked hard in drought. Not even all the manure and leaves we'd put there had made the clay into what Aunt Maura called "a good loamy soil." It was fertile, though. The vegetables all grew good, except for carrots and potatoes, which came out small and twisted from fighting against the clay.

The team lurched. The harness rattled. I could picture Aunt Maura back there bearing down on the plow to keep it driving through the crust. We made the turn at the end of the marked-out space and started back. The air smelled of the new-turned dirt, which lay in chunks and crescents along the furrow.

Uncle Ted was pitching the stones to the left, along the line for a wall. Smaller ones he threw with a quick turning of his wrist. The large, flat ones he picked up with his hands and heaved in a low arc.

He had added some weight during the past month, so that his blue shirt fitted him now. So did the spare green one which he had brought rolled up in his pack. He'd had Aunt Maura trim up his hair to collar length, and when he worked, like now, he tied a rolled-up bandanna around his head. The gash on his forehead was just an ugly scar now, which his hair mostly hid. His eyes were still bright and alert, and he never seemed easy. Even when he dozed by the fire he would wake up suddenly and look around, watching.

"Left! Turn them left, Neena, they're straying," Aunt Maura called. I tugged on Heidi's halter lead and got her headed back.

By the time the sun was straight up and we could break for lunch, we had a good section turned. The edges of the clods were dry and whitened from the air.

We washed most of the dirt off, our hands freezing from the coldness of the well water and the air, which wasn't yet as warm as the sun. When we were inside, Uncle Ted took off his shirt and hung it on a hook in the entryway because it was covered with dirt from handling stones.

I set the table with bread and slices of the last of the winter onions, and a bowl of new greens dressed with bacon grease and vinegar. There was milk, now, though the calf took its share.

"I'll be glad when the garden crops start coming on," Aunt Maura said.

"I'm tired of dried things and pickled things," I added. "Everything tastes sour."

"Be glad you've got as good as this," Uncle Ted put in. "I've seen families move back into the suburbs of Washington in the winter, just so they could hunt for canned goods in the houses and supermarkets. Knowing that the gangs and the scavengers have cleaned out everything worth having."

"Aren't they afraid of the metachemicals still being active?" Aunt Maura said.

"Uh-huh," he answered, through a mouthful of bread. "But it's that or starvation. They don't know how to grow food, don't have seeds or tools, and so far as eating off the land—they don't know pokeberries from huckleberries."

"It doesn't seem right to be planting corn for liquor when there's people starving," she said.

"Everything you could raise and spare wouldn't feed more than one family."

"Even so."

"Even so, people need their liquor, too. Just for the comfort of it."

"The comfort of getting drunk."

"Oh, Maura Lee," he said, in that kind of little-brother voice that made her smile. "Just think, with good pure alcohol, you'll be able to make some tinctures and extracts from your herbs."

"I'll leave that to the people who buy them, thank you," she said crisply. "It's enough trouble to pick and sort and dry and bundle them now."

A breadcrumb fell from Uncle Ted's mouth and rolled down his chest until it lodged in the red, curling hairs there. He brushed it aside, but saw me watching him.

"You ever hear people say that work will put hair on your chest?" he said.

I nodded.

"Well, you'd better watch out. Your aunt shouldn't work you so hard, Neena, or you'll grow up to look more like me," he said, patting his chest, "than like a woman."

A blush spread across my face. I put my head down and ate.

"Don't be telling her stories," Aunt Maura said. "She's starting to fill out some, though I'd say she'll always be skinny like Terra. Won't ever have any hips or breasts to amount to anything."

I blushed more to hear her say that to Uncle Ted. I wondered if she had seen me sometimes, feeling my new curves through my clothes. And I wondered if he had seen.

They went back to talking about his plan to make liquor. He was concerned about the water, what kind of stone it ran through. I couldn't look up at them, not even when the blush faded away. I ate another whole piece of bread, though I wasn't hungry.

Finally they were through eating, and I followed them back outside to finish plowing.

Sunny balked at being harnessed, swinging his blocky head and short horns from side to side, and what was strange was that the gentle Heidi acted just like him. She stepped backward into the chains, tangling them and cutting her leg.

"Spring's getting to them," Aunt Maura said, half out of breath from battling the two into harness. Once yoked and ready, though, they settled down. They made an odd-looking team

—Heidi, brown as a deer and her hipbones sticking up sharp, and Sunny, a sort of a gray-brindled white, shorter but heavy through the body.

The plowing went as smoothly as in the morning. Aunt Maura shouted commands to the team, and I tugged and talked Heidi wide on the turns and straight along the furrows. I passed Uncle Ted each time as he followed the plow. Once or twice he looked up and smiled with those beautiful white teeth, flashing out of the red of his beard like white fire out of coals.

We were near the end of the plowing when, on one of those meetings, he threw something toward me.

"Catch," he said.

I reached out my free hand and caught the little thing as it came end over end through the air. I felt the earth gritting back and forth between my fingers and the smooth surface of whatever it was.

I opened my hand and saw that it was a little figure, a round-bodied doll made out of plastic that was etched with scratches from the soil, and the color was nearly all bleached away. The face could still be seen, a sleeping baby face with dark curls and red spots for cheeks.

We were the last ones to get on the truck. We sat back by the tailgate, next to the soldiers with the guns on their shoulders. Mom had a little case of things she had carried, and I held our coats and Tiny Sarah, my doll.

"Where are we going?" I whispered to Mom. I
didn't want the soldiers to be angry. The one who
sat across from us was a black man. He was very
thin, and he wore his helmet shield down even in
the truck so that there was a light-shimmer where
his face should have been.

"Hagerstown. First to Frederick. Where Angeline
goes in the summer, to her grandparents' house."

"Why does Angeline have grandparents?"

"Because Angeline's mother chose to get married." She looked at the soldier sitting next to her,
but he was staring out over the tailgate.

"Oh."

I watched the reflections on the black soldier's
shield for a while, red reflections from the taillight,
which showed through a hole in the truck body.
There were trucks ahead of us, but there weren't
any following. On the roads there were just these
trucks loaded with people, all going out of the city
and none going in. The road was dark, like the
parking lot of the shopping center where we had
gotten on the trucks. There had been a lot more
people waiting there. They came up to the truck
and tried to climb on. The soldiers held their guns
down and told them "Wait for the next convoy."

We rode. There were people sitting on the floor
and more people standing. Everyone leaned backward as we started to climb, and I was pressed
against the soldier.

"Look," he said to the black soldier. He pointed
back through the dark. The black soldier lifted his
shield and the red taillight slid across his eye and
cheek as he leaned forward.

The place that was Baltimore was as dark as the

fields, except for lines of light that reached up from the ground, moving back and forth. In a minute I realized that the lights came down from the sky.

"Gunships," said the soldier beside me.

"Heavy Martines. Look like out of Charleston," said the black soldier.

"Full complement."

The lights swept across the city, and I could see the outlines of tall buildings when they were lit for a moment by the helicopter lights. When I rode in a helicopter with my Mom, we landed on top of a tower near the water. I wondered if the tower was one of the buildings I could see.

Then the lights, which had seemed so clear and perfect, began to get hazy and spread out.

"Dropped their load," the black soldier said.

"Bastards."

The haze grew, like smoke from a fire that covered all the city, and then the helicopter lights began to move out of Baltimore, up the dark road that we were on.

"I sure hope they're just getting out of the drift to regroup," said the soldier on our side.

"Don't think they'll hit Frederick. Least not tonight—they're empty for sure after that dump."

"I hope you're right. I got my family in Frederick."

"My family's back there," the black soldier said, still looking toward the city. "On Charles Street," and he dropped the shield over his face again.

"Neena?"

"She's having one of her fits."

"Is she sick?"

"She's remembering."

I felt something wet against my cheek. I stepped back and felt the ground give way under my feet, and I fell. Then the night all left me and it was daytime.

"You all right?" asked Uncle Ted, bending over to help me back up.

"Sure. I'm fine." I shook some of the dirt out of my clothes. I still had the little doll in my hand. I put it in my pocket.

"Heidi put her nose on you," Aunt Maura said. "Did she scare you?"

"No," I said, telling the truth.

Chapter Four

I DIDN'T THINK we'd ever see another renaissance.

I had read as far as the Italian Renaissance in a book that Aunt Maura had me studying called *History and World Cultures*. That Renaissance seemed so far away, and unlikely. After the Dark Ages, the rebirth.

We were in another dark age, Aunt Maura said. She also said it was important that people not forget, and that young people learn about the past. "You'll see the new renaissance coming," she said. "One empire falls and new ones are born." But it didn't seem likely.

All I had to do was look at the things which were set aside in a corner of the basement, the old video sets and the computer, stacked there with their blue screens covered with cobwebs and dust. Even I could see that it wasn't like when the Roman Empire fell. Then, people just went on with their horses and carts, using the roads and tearing down columns and aqueducts to build their barns. Just going on. But where would the power come from that used to make those screens glow and pictures move across them? Where would there be enough people, and materials, to create new cities, or the peace to build them?

It didn't seem likely.

I looked at the half-page illustration. "The Annunciation (detail) by Antonello Da Messina, 1474." The woman's eyes stared back at me as if I were the angel, and one hand was raised up as if she were greeting or maybe holding something away. Even though the paper was worn, the blue of her veil was rich and her skin glowed with a round golden light. Her lips were tilted, just a little. Maybe she had been caught laughing at something, and now with the angel she was nearly solemn. But her eyes were so calm, brown and deep.

I looked across the page and out the window.

The trees were fully green now, green getting deeper and deeper toward black the farther you looked into the forest, every leaf perfect and edged. June wasn't like August, when the air makes everything look blue. Then, the hills seemed to melt into the sky in the afternoons.

In the meadow, daisies were blooming.

The wind was from the southwest, calling up a storm. The leaves on the maple and tulip poplar trees were turned inside out, pale green, like a reflection of the clouds to come.

Aunt Maura would be back long before the clouds massed up and rain threatened. She had left that morning with her pack filled with bundles and bags of herbs to trade to the barterman for the things on the list that Ted had made.

"Copper," he told her, writing it down. "Sheet copper. Or tin, if you can't get that. And soft copper tubing, an inch in diameter."

He held the stub of the pencil straight up and down in his fingers as he wrote. The metal was what the blacksmith would need to make the distillery unit, the "still." Everything else, he said, we had right here, wood and corn and water.

"You really should come with me, Ted," said Aunt Maura, frowning as she looked at the little picture he had drawn beside his list. "I can't tell the barterman much about what you're doing."

He pressed his lips together and shook his head once from side to side. "I'll not go near him, sister."

"That's foolish."

"Then it's foolish."

He added a line to his drawing. His fingers were trembling. She stared at him. He bore down on the pencil and darkened the edge of one section, carefully, knowing that she was watching.

"There you go, Maura Lee," he said, grinning and waiting for her to smile in return. "A diagram even a fool could follow." When she didn't smile, his eyes darted away and he stopped smiling, too.

She shrugged and picked up the brown paper. The other side had a line or two in her cramped handwriting, small below other, crossed-out words, ordinary things we needed that the barterman might have. She folded the paper and put it in the pocket of her pants.

The metal, if she could get what he wanted, would then go to the blacksmith. Uncle Ted had walked down to the forge a week ago to talk with him and show him his diagrams. Old Matheney had " 'lowed as how he could cobble up something like," Uncle Ted had reported, mocking the old man's slow talk and South Counties accent.

He was sitting on the porch outside the window, rocking back and forth in the chair, making the floorboards creak so that I started to read in rhythm with the squeak-squeak, squeak-squawk. I imagined that he was still watching the ridge path that Aunt Maura had taken. He was smoking—the tobacco smoke drifted in the window when the breeze backed around. He did so truly love to smoke that right after he came, Aunt Maura had traded high to get him some leaf from the barterman.

"You're an expensive luxury," she said when

she handed him the little cloth-wrapped bundle, a surprise.

He put his arm around her tired shoulders. "But little brothers aren't so easy to find these days." And she had smiled right open, a smile like I couldn't ever remember her giving to me.

I pulled my thoughts back to the book. The painters of the Renaissance.

"What're you doing, Neena?"

I called back through the open window, "Studying."

The rocking chair squeaked hard, once, and then I heard Uncle Ted walking to the door. He came in and went behind me, leaning his arms on the back of my chair.

"Where did your aunt get that musty thing?"

"I don't know."

He picked it up. "History. Dead history. No wonder you short your lessons."

"I do not."

"I don't blame you." He tossed the book back on the table and went over to the shelves.

He kneeled and pulled out the books, one at a time. The first was Aunt Maura's herbal, its worn back stitched together and the whole thing crammed with other pages and drawings she had added. The other books weren't nearly as well used. Most of their spines were blackened by mildew, some by smoke, and the titles could not be read. Some of them I knew Aunt Maura had bargained for, trading the barks and roots we gathered for old words in old books.

"Botany," he muttered. "Grammar. These are

all textbooks. Doesn't she have a thing to read but textbooks?"

"There are more books in the herb room," I said. "They're in a chest. I don't know what they are."

Uncle Ted pushed a thick book back into place and stood. He put his hand on my shoulder. "Let's go see."

The herb room was thick with the medicinals we had already gathered. There were trays of slippery elm and dogwood bark drying, set up on bricks off the floor, and bundles of meadowsweet hung from the rafters. Flagroot was piled on a piece of cloth. The air was half spicebark fragrant, half foul. I took a box of old, powdery boneset off the chest and the powder flew up and glowed in the light coming in the window.

Uncle Ted pried back the latch, breaking off flakes of rust, and opened the chest. More dust flew up. He brushed aside some spiderwebs and the cocoons of moths, pulled out an old ragged shawl, and picked up one of the books that was hidden underneath.

"*Lord Jim*," he said. He picked up another, reading, "*The Return of the Native*."

"What are those?"

"Novels. Fiction."

"Things that aren't real?"

"These things are more real than that history book you're reading, Neena," he said earnestly. "The people in these books are alive." He leaned down into the chest and rummaged around.

"Here," he said, coming up surrounded by a thin cloud, like smoke. He had a large book in his hand. "You want to learn about the Italian Renaissance?"

I didn't, really, but I didn't say anything.

He hit the cover twice, knocking away the film of dust. He opened it up and began to read in a slow, measured voice.

> *"Midway upon the journey of my life*
> *I found that I was in a dusky wood;*
> *For the right path, whence I had strayed, was lost.*
> *Ah me! How hard a thing it is to tell*
> *The wildness of that rough and savage place . . ."*

He held the book up and the light caught a gleam of gold from the page edges. "This is Dante's *Divine Comedy*. This is the Renaissance."

I remembered reading about Dante. Somehow, I had thought the things he had written had been lost, along with all the other things put down by the people who lived in what Uncle Ted called "dead history."

He handed me the book, and holding it I felt as if I had some connection to that long-ago time. These words had survived through all the wars, words about being lost in a wild place. I knew that feeling.

"The words . . ." I said, not knowing how to explain.

"It's poetry, Neena. Not Dante's poetry, because he wrote in another language, but a translation." He closed the lid on the trunk and we sat down. The warm air came through the open window and brushed across our backs.

"This is the story of a journey through Hell,

and Purgatory and Paradise," he explained. "Do
you know about those?"

I nodded. At least, I knew what Hell and Paradise were.

"There are three sections, and those three are
divided into cantos, or songs." He opened the
book and showed me the first page where he
had read. The opposite page showed a man in a
robe, surrounded by trees and vines and
shadows. "Dante astray in the Dusky Wood."

> *"After my weary body had been rested,*
> *Again I started up the desert steep,*
> *So that my lower foot was e'er the firmer.*
> *When lo! Close to the bottom of the mount,*
> *A leopardess, light-poised and passing swift,*
> *Her hide all covered o'er with inky spots!*
> *She always stood before me, face to face,*
> *Blocking my path whenever I advanced,*
> *So that I turned and turned again in vain."*

I followed where he read, each line ending
and returning, and the words rhythmic as the
sound of the rocking chair on the porch.

"Is the whole book about the woods and the
animals?"

"No. Oh, no," he said, half-laughing. "What he
wrote was a kind of a dream. According to this
poem, Dante was in danger of losing his soul
when he was guided on this path. That's what
the book is about, traveling through the three
supernatural regions so that he will be healed.
Here, look."

I took the spread book into my lap and turned

the pages. There was a dark drawing of Dante, and his guide, Virgil. Both of them had wreaths of leaves around their heads. Virgil, I remembered reading once, was from the Roman time. And there was a drawing of huddled, naked people being herded into a little boat on a black river.

"These are souls, people condemned to Hell," Uncle Ted explained. "As he walks through Hell, Dante will talk with them, about their punishment but also about the people and politics of Italy in his time. You'll learn more about the Renaissance here than in any textbook."

I turned the pages, away from the poor tormented people, and started to read to myself in Canto 5.

> I said to him, 'O poet, I would speak
> To that sequestered pair that cling together
> And seem to float so lightly on the wind.'
> He answered me: 'Take heed when they approach
> More nearly to us: ask them by that love
> Which bears them on, and they will come to you.'

"Se . . . questered?" I asked. I could understand more words than I knew how to pronounce, from reading, but this one was new.

"Sequestered. Set apart," he answered, then urged, "Read it aloud, Neena. It's the only way to really understand the movement of the poetry, to say it out loud."

I began to read, halting on the difficult words, the names from that distant place and time. I began to feel the sway of the lines.

"And she replied: 'There is no greater grief
Than to recall a bygone happiness
In present misery: that your teacher knows.
But if you have so great a wish to learn
The very root whence sprang our sinful love,
I'll tell our tale, like one who speaks and weeps.

'One day to pass the time, we read the book
Of Launcelot, and how love conquered him.
We were all unsuspecting and alone:
From time to time our eyes would leave the page
And meet to kindle blushes in our cheeks.
But at one point alone we were o'ercome:
When we were reading how those smiling lips
Were kissed by such a lover—Paolo here,
Who nevermore from me shall be divided,
All trembling, held and kissed me on the mouth.
Our Galeot was the book; and he that wrote it,
A Galeot! On that day we read no more.'"

I turned the page, hurriedly, feeling the blush
mounting up on my face, and there was a drawing of a white naked woman held by a man, his
head leaning on her shoulder and her face
turned back toward him with a look all soft and
surrendered. Her long hair and loose robe
streaming in the winds of Hell. And I turned
that page.

"You don't need to be embarrassed, Neena,"
he said. "Here."

I looked up, then down again.

"History, all that dried-up stuff, was lived by
people like us. Like these. But the history
writers squeezed every person they ever wrote

about into a suit of clothes and a name. No life at all." I looked at him again and saw that his face was golden in the light through the window, and as he spoke he shook his head and his hair glinted gold. "That's why this is real. Real people, feeling."

The book slid off my lap and thumped on the floor, closed. I leaned away from him and picked it up.

"Your aunt! She chose to shut herself off from men and from children, a long time ago. From everybody. She shouldn't do that to you. You've been here—how long?"

"More than eight years."

"And how many people have you seen in that time?"

I thought. Ditsky-the-Peddler. Old Mr. Hollis and his three grown daughters. A few of the people who came themselves after remedies, standing restlessly at the door until Aunt Maura handed them the medicine and then they were gone.

"I thought so." He took my chin in his big hand. "Neena."

And he looked at me, and his blue eyes became dreamy and far away, and he seemed to lose the words that he was going to say.

"Oh, Neena." He put his hand on my head and stroked my hair down to my shoulders. His lips were parted a little, like the man's in the book, and I could see the white of his teeth. "You're a lovely girl, Neena, too lovely to be living in these times."

His eyes focused on something very far away,

the little crow's-foot lines crinkling at the corners as if he were straining to see something. His hands were warm on my hair and my face. Warmth that flowed right through me, warmth like the sun baking my bones in July. My skin prickled on my arms.

I had been a woman, according to Aunt Maura, for nearly two years, since I had started to bleed each month. I could feel myself changing, my body changing, but I wondered if this feeling, too, went with being a woman. One part of me kept saying that this was the loving that I had just read about, while the other part kept repeating, louder, that it could not be because he was kin.

I felt something very close to the surface, wanting to cry. Or wanting to laugh and breathe in the warmth and the gold in the air.

He shook his head and his eyes cleared. He took the book from my lap and he stood up, then gave me his hand and I stood beside him.

"My sister may not like it, but I think it's time your education was in something more than textbooks. Since we've started with Dante, we'll stay with it," he said.

We went out of the herb room and closed the door behind us.

Until Aunt Maura came home and the evening came in on a gathering rainstorm, I kept hearing that one line, my own voice reading, "On that day we read no more."

Chapter Five

———◆———

THE MORNING WAS sweet and cool, a morning
which seemed more like one in late spring than
fall. There were little patches of fog resting between the hills and white in the river valley. The
rounds of spiderwebs showed everywhere in the
brown grass, among the bushes in the fencerow.
There was even one strung pearl-by-pearl between the stair railing and the porch post. But
the trees flaming red and yellow reminded me
that summer was gone away, as surely as the
Hunter climbing in the night sky.

The cornfield stretched away behind the barn,
yellow-ripe in the stalks and in the cobs. It was
time to cut the corn and bring it in.

I leaned over the railing and touched the web,
hoping that the big yellow-and-black spider
would think it was a grasshopper and come running across her web, but the strand broke
against my finger and the spider stayed hidden.

In the kitchen, I could hear Aunt Maura building up the fire in the stove, getting water to
make coffee from the tall stone crock I'd already
filled. That was my first chore every morning, to
carry in water from the well. Uncle Ted was
walking around the kitchen, his footsteps heavy,
and then he began to whistle. It was a happy
tune that ran up and down, repeating. It
sounded like the fiddle tune I'd heard a man
play once, a man resting by the side of the hard
road.

"You're sounding cheery this morning," she said, her voice muffled.

"Today we put in the corn, and then I'll make the whiskey." He whistled a few notes. "The whiskey will be barter for a fine roan mare with a black tail and four white socks," he said, then, seeing me come in, pointed at me and sang, "and on that roan mare I'll take Neena there for a ride round every ridge."

"And we'll find gold under the broken bridge!" I sang back, proud of the rhyme.

"Daneen!"

I ducked my head. "Sorry, Aunt Maura." She was always grouchy early in the morning.

"Easy, Maura Lee."

"Well, enough of your talk about gold—and about fancy horses, for that matter. We could better use some tools here, to say nothing of the necessities. The cost of making that still has about taken up my medicinals for the year to the barterman."

"Next fall we'll make a real profit. We'll get you a white plow horse to ride," he teased.

"And how about a jackass for you?"

Uncle Ted winked at me and then sat down at the table. He leaned back in the chair and watched while we went around getting the dishes and food.

They kept at each other during breakfast, Uncle Ted "instigating," as Aunt Maura called it, and her enjoying the fun and trying not to let it show.

By the time we got to the field, the sun was

over the ridge and the dew was drying. We made the corn leaves, brown with some of the top ones still showing some green, rattle as we walked at the edge of the field.

We started at the far end of the field. Uncle Ted had made up a sort of heavy, curved knife from a broken leaf spring on the old truck, grinding the edge down and setting it into a wooden handle. He used the knife to cut the cornstalks. Aunt Maura and I came behind, tying the stalks into bundles of ten, then tying a dozen bundles into shocks, which we set up in the row.

Aunt Maura stripped back the dried husks on some of the ears. It was mostly good corn, long and solid, some of the kernels yellow and some white, and some mixed with red. The tips of the kernels were dented in. It had been a good year for corn, after a wet spring. No smut, and not very many earworms.

His knife cracked through the tough stalks. The ears thumped as they hit the ground, rattled in the husks. Our binding made its own crisp sound, and when we set the shock together there was the sound of two hundred ears settling against each other.

Uncle Ted, getting ready to start a new row, stopped and stripped off his shirt. He threw it across the fence.

Crack. Thump. Crackle, crackle. Thump. I started thinking of poems that matched the rhythm. The meter, Uncle Ted called it, the feet that marched in time. Our feet shuffled down the dry between-rows of the cornfield. Crack, thump.

Uncle Ted, a space lengthened out between us by his steady cutting, stopped and retied the bandanna around his head.

I watched him working. His back muscles flexed as he struck his knife through the cornstalk, and as he pulled it free. I could see the little knobs of his spine moving under his skin, which was mostly tanned and freckled, still a little red on his neck and shoulders where he had worked for a long time yesterday in the sun, repairing the fence. Sweat shone on his skin and matted his hair into dark points on his neck.

I wondered if he would buy a horse, like he said. A horse would let us get around to places, into that little corner of Middletown where the blacksmith and the barrel-maker and other craftspeople lived, around to the farms other than the Hollises. You just couldn't go fast behind an ox team. Though I suppose you could go far if you had long enough.

If Uncle Ted had had to walk, it must have taken him a long time to come across the mountains from the coast. He never talked about it, though, so maybe he had a horse sometimes.

I thought about him mounted up on a tall horse, its tail swishing nearly to the ground. And I could get up behind him and ride farther than I had ever seen. But it should be a white horse, not a roan, because then he would look something like I thought the knight Launcelot must look, from the stories we had read.

Since that day when we found the books in the old trunk, I hadn't opened another textbook. There were twenty-six books in that trunk, old romantic ones and novels printed just before the wars started, books that were mostly sad and full of unhappy people. Together, we had read through the tales of King Arthur's Court, and some of the plays by Shakespeare out of a heavy book with thin, fragile paper, and *Ivanhoe*. The Arthur stories were my favorite. Sometimes I'd just repeat the long names to myself: Lancelot, Guinevere, Gawain, Percival, Elaine the Lily Maid of Astolat, Galahad. They were poems all by themselves, drumming like the hoofbeats of the horses in the battles they fought.

He must have had to fight, coming across the mountains. That's where he'd gotten the gash on his forehead. There were raiders, and watchers on the borders, and people who were afraid of strangers. Like we all were.

I imagined Uncle Ted backed up against a tree on a mountainside, late in the evening, slashing away at shadowy attackers.

The knife chunked against a stalk close in front of me, and I jumped.

"Sorry, Neena. I didn't mean to scare you."

He threw the knife down and crouched to be at my level. "Were you remembering again?"

"No." I brushed my hair away from my eyes and felt the sweat gathering on the back of my neck. Aunt Maura was far ahead of me, binding up a sheaf, and Uncle Ted had already made the turn and was chopping near where I stood.

His sweat smelled different from mine, or Aunt Maura's. Stronger, but a good smell, like the foam on a horse after it's been run.

He took off his bandanna, dark red with sweat, mopped the back of his hand across his forehead and then tied it back. He was all slick with sweat, and his chest and arms were blackened with dust and the trash off the silks and tassels.

"Well, I had better get moving—and so should you," he said. He lifted the knife and swung it, thwack, dividing a stalk from its roots.

I ran and caught up with Aunt Maura. I felt bad because she was red-faced from bending and working, while I'd been daydreaming.

The field was stubbled with the ends of the corn. The shocks, now beginning to look like an accomplishment, would provide fodder for the cattle when the ear corn was stripped off. Husks could be used as stuffing for mattresses or in starting fires.

It was steady work right through until lunch. Uncle Ted never seemed to tire out, and with him working, we had to keep up. It wouldn't do to leave the field for another day. The weather was changeable this time of year. Ready corn, left standing, might fall over in a windstorm and be soaked in the mud.

We cleaned up quick and ate a lunch of bread and cold, roasted rabbit. We drank a lot to wash the dust out of our throats. Then we went back to the field.

It was hard to have that same enthusiasm as in the morning. I had little cuts all over my arms and face from the edges of the dry leaves. There was dust and filth all down my back, itching with sweat. My thumb hurt where I'd rammed a stalk splinter under the nail. I wished I could be like Aunt Maura, who hadn't started the day so eager but who seemed to wear through it all. She just worked, quiet and bent over, almost like all the years of work were layered up on her like callus, making her heavy and slow.

Second thought, I didn't want to get that way.

My cotton gloves were dirty and torn through at the fingers, and my hands ached from holding and tying and bundling. I could feel blisters on the soft places on my palms. I could feel raw places on my fingertips.

Uncle Ted, as he got close to the end of the field, cut faster. His knife chunked into each stalk. Then he was at the end of the last row. He cut the last stalk, threw it up in the air and caught it.

"Finished!" he shouted.

Aunt Maura straightened up and looked at him. "Harvest's home," she said. "Save the ears from that stalk—we'll put them up over the door."

"Sure you don't want to sacrifice it to the Grain Mother?" he said.

"Oh, Ted. I just like to look up and see that last corn, come winter. To remember the season."

"Sure." But his knife chunked, twice, and he threw two ears to the side of the field anyway.

We worked along faster now. The day was ending. The evening star was bright over the ridge, and on the horizon to the north was the edge of a purple front of clouds. The breeze had shifted around and was cool from the north.

Uncle Ted went and got his shirt and put it on. Then he came and helped us bind up the rest of the sheaves and the shocks. When the last one was finished, we stood back and looked over the naked field. The clouds were bigger, a broad band preceded by a few long wisps.

"A good day's work, Ted."

"A hell of a day's work," he answered. He put his hands on each side of his back and bent back until his spine cracked. "I haven't worked like that since . . ."

He didn't finish.

"I wouldn't have looked for such a harvest, after April and May being so wet and cold," I put in.

Aunt Maura laughed. "You sound like the image of me."

"No way does she look it," Uncle Ted answered.

"No," she said, "no, that's true."

The corn shocks were pale against the field, like people, standing and waiting, wrapped in pale cloaks.

"What do you think this harvest will bring?" Aunt Maura said slowly.

"How many bushels do you figure?"

"Well, I'd say we'll get better than forty

bushels of shelled corn. Take away seed corn for next year, and the corn you'll need for malt, and Conaway's payment for the milling. We have to have some meal for our own use, so say sixteen to seventeen bushels of meal left for your distilling."

Uncle Ted did some quick figuring. "About fifty gallons of prime liquor, after it's cut back with water."

That didn't seem like a lot for all the tilling and hoeing, and the harvesting we'd just done. But then, Uncle Ted had told us that good liquor was as valuable as the best herbs we could gather, and the barterman had told Aunt Maura the same thing. I'd never tasted any, good or bad, or even seen any that I knew.

"What do you think, Neena?" he said. "Worth the sore back?"

"I don't know."

"If this barterman you deal with is fair at all —and I've known of ones, and not Changes, either, that weren't close to honest—we should be living well come next fall. Why, whiskey like this, that won't turn you sick or blind—it's worth its weight in ..."

"Ammunition and kerosene, I hope," Aunt Maura said, dampening down his excitement.

"Hey, Maura Lee, you're allowed to feel good." I saw his hand, white at the end of his sleeve, go around her shoulders and draw her in for a big, work-dirty hug. I stood on the other side of them, wishing that I was in that hug, too.

The day was gone, all but a last faint-red glow in the west and on the edges of the clouds layering up across the northern quarter of the sky. We walked back to the house in the dark, Uncle Ted with his arm still around his sister's shoulders, and him humming a piece of that same tune he'd started in the morning.

I poked up the fire in the stove and caught a light on the end of a kindling splinter. Uncle Ted lifted the globe on the lantern, and I touched the flame to the wick. It lit up tall on one side, then spread across the wick and burned high, guttering and smoking. I put my hand on the knob to turn it down, and his hand was already there.

I looked up. His eyes were bright blue and shining in the high flame, and his cheeks were red from the work in the wind. He put his tongue out and moistened his lips. His eyes were steady, and they didn't dart away.

He slipped his fingers free from under mine and let me adjust the wick.

My heart was beating away, loud as if I had run the ridge. I watched him set the globe back on the lantern and lift the lantern to hang it on the wall. He fiddled with the bent reflector on the back. All the time, he was looking at me. I saw a tiny reflection of myself on his eyes, my own invisible blue eyes looking back at him.

I went in to the bedroom I shared with Aunt Maura. I poured some water into the washpan and wiped off most of the dirt in the dark. Then I undressed and laid down on the bed, with the sheet up over me and the blankets over my feet.

"Daneen?" Aunt Maura called.

"I'm in bed."

She came and opened the door and stood

there, just a black shadow against the light in the other room. "Are you sick? Do you have a fever?"

"No. I'm just tired." I pulled one blanket up to my chin.

"Don't you want any dinner?"

"No. Not really. Unless you need me to help fix something."

"Oh, no. We'll just pick a little. We'll have a good breakfast in the morning. You'll feel like it then."

"Yes, Aunt Maura. Good night."

"Good night."

I lay there for the longest time, it seemed, hearing them talking as they sat at the kitchen table. Then Aunt Maura came in and got ready for bed. She took off her field clothes and washed, carefully, hardly splashing a bit. Then she pulled on her long, blue gown. She lay down and the springs squeaked under her as she turned over, finding a comfortable place.

Last of all, Uncle Ted got up from the table. I heard him check the fire that Aunt Maura had banked. He went outside and came back, then took a drink from the jar. He put out the light and went up the ladder to his loft, which was right above our bedroom.

I heard him moving around up there for a while, then he lay down and the floor made a little sound as his weight settled on the bed.

I thought about getting up and getting a drink, or washing my face off again. It was the windburn that made it hot as fire. I pushed back the blanket and as I did I ran my hands down over the swell of my breasts, my stomach and the round of my hips. My skin was warm and smooth. I felt like I'd been running naked in the wind, and all my skin was windburned and warm and pink.

Chapter Six

———•———

Arden's Diary
Oct. 15

I HAVE BURIED the body of Tom Decker in the corner of the back meadow, where it comes against the old road.

I did him the honor of wrapping his body in a clean piece of sheeting before I laid it in the hole. He did not deserve the death he found, nor did the woman and two young children who were with him deserve to be left companionless as well as homeless and hungry.

The woman told me his name, but refused to tell me hers. She believes, I am certain, that I killed Tom Decker, though I do not know how she has justified, to herself, my carrying the body two miles and burying it properly. It was enough for her to see my altered face and form —those could explain any monstrosity. She and the children sat under an oak tree and watched me dig the grave and then cover the body with earth. They did not cry, nor did they perform any small rituals such as throwing in a handful of earth. Then they stood up and walked away down the old road, carrying the boots and belt which had been Tom Decker's, the older boy wearing his hat.

I would say that they were casual acquaintances, met on the road, but they may well have been a family.

I told the woman that he had been killed while trying to steal food from a neighboring farm. She accepted that the way she accepted my presence—without enough energy to hate or even fear. She had the most lusterless gray eyes, absolutely dull, like her whole face worn by life.

I did not tell her who the killer was.

She will trade off Decker's memory with his boots and belt. But I won't be able to forget the way he died.

I had walked up on the ridge east of my home, wanting to check a grove of butternut trees there. I found a good crop of nuts, their long shells distinguishing them from the round husks of a few scattered walnuts, which lay among them. As I stood there, among the fallen leaves, I saw two people running across Maura Daucherty's back meadow.

I could not see them well, because of the ironweed and blackberry briers that had grown up in the field. They dodged among these clumps. I could see that the second person appeared to be gaining on the first.

I would not have interfered, except that I was

concerned for Maura and her niece. I worked my way down the ridge on a line to intercept the runners.

The greenbrier tangled around my ankles, the thorns biting into cloth and twisting fast. The entire slope was covered with the vines, leaves red and yellow and the berries a glossy dark blue among them. I fought through without much concern for noise.

When the trees opened at the edge of the field, I stopped. There was no sound of running, but I could hear loud breathing near the fence.

I went left and came out in front of the sound. I was too late.

A blond-haired man was standing over the body, a crumpled pile of rags with only the hands showing white and fragilely human. A brown slouch hat, very stained and worn, had rolled aside and rested upside down by one hand. The fingers on that hand moved once, relaxing from their clutch against the earth, and were still.

The blond man looked up and saw me—went pale, immediately, dead white under his tan. A scar showed livid across his forehead.

"Who was he?" I asked.

He said nothing. I saw that he held a knife in his hand. I did not unsheath the one that was at my belt, and I saw him focus on it, then quickly away.

"Why did you kill him?"

"You're the Change," he said, his voice trembling with his rapid breathing and also, I was certain, from fear.

"Yes." Under his stare I could feel every alteration that had come to my body. "But who is he?"

He looked down, momentarily. "He was stealing food. I caught him and I chased him. There's no crime in killing a thief."

I walked toward him and the blond man backed away, still holding the knife. Keeping an eye on the knife, I pushed the body over with the toe of my boot.

The man looked to be forty, forty-five maybe, though age is a very uncertain thing. When a man has been hungry for a long time, he looks older than he is, and this man had been hungry for a long time. His skin was sallow, and there were deep circles under his staring eyes. The veins stood out in his hands and throat. There was a little blood on his lips, but none elsewhere. The knife had entered from the back.

The dead man's hands were empty, and he wore no weapon. I felt a spasm of nausea.

It is not that I have not seen death and killing; I have walked past a hundred thousand destroyed bodies in the streets of Washington. I have seen decaying bodies left by the road. I myself have shot raiders without remorse, and seen my big dog, Lawyer, tear out the throat of a daring thief. These times do not allow for softness—but the blond man killed as a coward kills, out of fear, not necessity. Reasonless. The dead man had not taken a thing and was not a threat. He was simply hungry.

"You said he was stealing," I finally said.

"Trying to steal."

"He didn't get anything, then?"

"No," the blond man answered, sullen.

I looked at the body. A scavenger who had come in the night before had told of a family camping along the old road, and this man seemed to fit the description. He was ragged enough.

Then I looked back up at the blond man, back at his stare. "And who are you?"

"I have a right to be here," he said, truculently, then as I waited, "Ted Daucherty. Maura —I'm her brother."

"Ah."

Maura had been bartering things all summer for metal and pipe, so that this brother could distill alcohol for barter. I told her I'd take the whiskey—and meantime I had asked for information on the man. Trading out poison to people was not something I'd do.

The reports came back sporadically, each of them differing somewhat but in total adding up to an ugly truth.

Ted Daucherty had worked as a biochemist for the NordAmer military government, later switching allegiance to the Sutherland. When he had come into disfavor with the ruling families for some crime no one knew, he had drifted west. He'd been taken by the Pittsburgh Hierarchy, escaped field slavery by proving his talents, and worked for them until he either was released or escaped. He had come into this area from the north, on the old four-lane from Pittsburgh.

Looking at him, his head cocked forward as if he were already moving away, I felt again the agony of my bones and tissue in the days after the metachemicals had fallen on Washington. The planes that had dropped the bombs had been marked with the Sutherland's rayed sun and circle of stars. Everyone I knew had died, everyone on the campus, all my students, and all the other faculty members. Everyone in the block of apartments where I lived. Everyone it seemed but me, and I had suffered the agonies of hell while my flesh grew and altered and knit.

Ted Daucherty might well have fashioned those chemicals.

"You know something about this," I said at last, without other explanation than myself, standing before him.

"Why do you say that?" He kept his face turned half away, but I saw his eyes darting.

"I have scavengers moving from here to the coast, and north and south. I hear about people on the road. You came down from the north. From Pittsburgh."

"I came from the coast," he answered. "I lived on the Eastern Shore."

"A liar, too," I muttered, forgetting myself.

He rolled the knife handle in his hand and half crouched.

"You don't know anything," he said, pushing, anxious. Afraid.

Fear was the most dangerous of emotions.

I swallowed down my anger. There was nothing I could do to him that could ever repay what was done to me and others, yet he was only a small part of the whole. If, indeed, he was what people had said of him and what his actions indicated.

"This man was with a woman and two young children," I said.

He glanced down at the body and then, momentarily, wincing, at my face. Then he turned and began to walk back the way he had come. His back was stiff, as though he feared a knife.

I let him go. I picked up the body and took it to the road, stopping first to get the winding sheet. And then I told the nameless woman what had happened, and learned that his name was Tom Decker. In the winter, I may carve a wooden marker to replace the round stone that marks him now.

I have been lucky in having Maura as a neighbor, a woman of great sense and endurance. I have never seen the young girl who came to her, entrusted to a pack peddler's care, though I hear that she rather favors this uncle of hers. Who I admit I do not like at all.

This is enough for today. I will check my storerooms and then go to bed. The night is very quiet.

Chapter Seven

—◆—

I CARRIED TWO small collecting baskets. Aunt Maura, walking ahead of me, bristled like a porcupine with bundles of seven-barks root that she carried, and which were tied crosswise on her back. The twiggy roots brushed together and against the tree limbs as she walked.

The baskets I carried held ginseng and goldenseal root, each in its own basket. The goldenseal roots were knotty and yellow, the reason for the name. The plant had once been known as yellow puccoon. We could have brought in baskets full of goldenseal, and sold every bit, since preparations of the root were good not only against typhoid but also for diseases of the eye.

But ginseng, Aunt Maura said, was more reputation than fact. "People believe it'll cure nearly everything, from asthma to infertility," she often said. "I would say it has its uses, for stomach problems and the like, but as for the rest . . ." We dug it anyway, because we could sell it. And, as Aunt Maura also said, what people believed would do them good would often enough really do them good.

The fall was coming on fast, now, the leaves better than half down, others hanging loosely to the branches, twisting in the softest breeze until they came free and fell. The ground was covered with leaves. You could tell the kind of trees overhead just by the color—rock maple had bright red leaves with pink undersides, sugar maple was orange and yellow, beech was yellow, dogwood was maroon and ash was purplish. Walnut leaves had long since been down, and already had separated into brown leaflets and the long central stems.

There were fine shavings and shell halves under the hickory trees where squirrels had been working.

The collecting season was about over. Some roots you could dig right through January, especially seven-barks, which grew in thickets on the hillsides and old roadcuts. The flat flower heads dried and stayed on the branches, all winter. We usually quit collecting when the first "sticking" snow had arrived. Winter was when we rested, mended clothes, watched the sun go down early as it moved south and then slowly, slowly north through the bare trees.

The farm appeared sooner, now, with the woods opening up. First the bulk of the barn, with the cow trails brown in the yard around the watering trough, then the shed, the outhouse, finally the house. There was blue smoke coming up from the chimney, the thin smoke of a banked fire, and above where the springhouse run joined Littlefalls Creek, there was more smoke where Uncle Ted was working at his distillery.

"Smoke's rising straight," Aunt Maura said. "No rain likely."

We went across the stile into the back pasture and then cut across the corner toward the gate.

The sky was clear and blue, with a few wisps

of cloud in the west. It was a fine day, the sun warm and the air a little chill. I breathed in the smell of the smoke, and the fall taste of the leaves.

I balanced the weight of the baskets in my hands, the right-hand one with the ginseng a little heavier, and walked along lightly in the leaves. Fall and spring both made me pick up my feet like dancing, but for different reasons.

Heidi came around the barn with her calf. I had named it Sandy. It was a heifer calf, brown like Heidi but looking to be thicker through the body and shorter-legged than she was. The calf butted against her as she walked, wanting to suck, but Heidi kept walking until she was at the water tank and then she stood, drinking, and let the calf suck.

"Are we going to keep Sandy?" I asked.

"This winter."

"Not next year?"

"I'd like to have the calves from two cows, but that's a lot of winter fodder. I imagine we'll butcher her next fall."

We wouldn't have a beef to butcher this year. We had had to pull Heidi's calf last spring and it came dead, the birth blood and fluids shiny on its black coat. This winter, we'd have wild meat.

I ran in front of Aunt Maura and unhooked the chain that kept the gate closed between the pastures. I let her through and then fastened it behind us.

Sunny came up out of the woods, his big head swinging from side to side as he followed us. He thought that we had fodder. He pushed his wet nose against Aunt Maura's bundles and then backed off and stood, watching me.

"Git, Sunny!" I shooed him by shaking the baskets.

Heidi and the calf had to take a look, then the calf kicked away and she followed. She was wide-bellied already, fat from the summer and from the spring calf she carried. We went out of the field and came around the barn.

"Yoh!" The call caught us. "Yoh, Maura!"

"It's Ditsky!" I took hold of the basket handles tight and began to run.

"Don't spill that," she called after, but I was already halfway to the house, where the peddler waited on the porch.

He had his pack off and resting against a post; his knobbed walking stick lay on the ground. It looked like he had been there for a while.

"Princess," he said, and I ran up to him and he held out his arms. I started to run into his hug and then I slowed down and almost stopped. But he smiled just the same, that crooked grin, and I walked up and he hugged me.

"Lord, but you've grown," he said. "You're not a little princess anymore." He took me by the shoulders. "Were you this tall in the spring?"

"Yes."

"You're as tall as I am." And I was, just as tall.

Ditsky-the-Peddler was about the same age as Uncle Ted. He was thin from his walking, and he wore clothes and jewelry that he had traded for all along his route—shiny beads on a chain around his neck, a blue stone earring in one ear and a silver one in the other. He had black eyes, and he wore his black hair in a long braid that was tied sometimes with a bit of cloth but today with a leather string.

Aunt Maura came up. "Headed south, Ditsky?"

He put his hands at the small of his back and straightened his shoulders. "Yeah. Two nights ago I got caught in the open in a white frost. Winter's coming fast."

"It is that."

"You've been well here, then," he said. "You both look well."

"It's been a busy summer."

"Your brother still here?"

"Ted." And she nodded. It seemed like Ditsky's wide smile was a little less wide.

"Well, come on in. I want to set aside these gatherings and get us all something to drink."

They went in and I tailed after. Aunt Maura took my baskets, and while she got things laid out for drying in the herb room, I poked up the fire and set some water on to boil. Ditsky took the chair back in the corner, facing the door and the counter where I was working.

"Looking at you today, walking through the field beside your aunt, it doesn't seem possible that you're that little girl I brought across the mountains," he said.

"Aunt Maura said that hard work is good for growing."

"We've all got plenty of work, but I'm not growing any."

I laughed. I measured out the tisane that Aunt

Maura liked on afternoons after working, the one that had blackberry in it.

"You want coffee or tea?"

"What you're fixing for your aunt is fine."

"Okay."

I always was easy with Ditsky. Like family, Aunt Maura called him. He didn't seem to have aged at all in the years I'd known him. He still wore all his patches and strange things, and when he moved he made me think of a kind of loose-jointed doll. And he still called me Princess.

The pot began to hum with the water heating. Aunt Maura came out of the drying room and shut the door, which sent vibrations through the floor under my feet.

She came in, dusting her hands off on her pants, and sat down across the table from him.

"Well, Ditsky, what's the news from around?"

"Old Mister Carella has buried his second grandchild. Diphtheria."

"That heavy boy—John?"

"That one."

Aunt Maura clucked.

"The Efaw girl, Colleen I think her name is, is married to Bosker Thomas. At least, she's taken his name, though I don't think there was any ceremony like her mother is trying to put on. She's pregnant, real big."

They talked while I brewed the tea. Some of the people I knew from the few times we had gone into Middletown. Mister Carella was the shoemaker. The Efaws made barrels and the Thomases lived by a little farming, a lot of hunting and, some people said, by thieving. Other ones I'd only heard talked about. Ditsky, of course, knew everybody.

"What about back East?" Aunt Maura asked, quietly.

"About the same. About the same." He shook his head and the braid brushed across his shoulders. "There's still some fighting going on, but most of the coastal areas and wide spans around the cities have been abandoned. The metachemicals spreading around in the runoff, you know. The scavengers go in, and there are some of the crazy and some of the desperate there, too. There are a lot of wild folk on the roads."

"Aren't you afraid?" I asked.

He looked at me and winked. Then he put his hand down inside his shirt and pulled out a little red bag on a string.

"I met an Indian woman. She was a Cherokee, she said, going with her family to take their land back in the Carolinas. She wanted some fine wire that I had, and she didn't have anything I wanted in trade, so she made me this medicine bag against my troubles."

"What's in it?"

He felt the little bag with his fingers. "A little bone of some kind, and something that feels like a forked twig. Something soft. She told me never to open it up or the magic would get out."

He dropped the bag back inside the neck of his shirt and patted his chest where it lay. "I haven't been sick since I put this on, nor have I been troubled on the road."

We drank some tea. Aunt Maura and Ditsky talked more in that short way that people have who know each other, just a word or two.

"What've you brought us?" Aunt Maura said at last.

"Things sharp and things soft," he said. "I made a good trade up Riverway for needles, thread. And cloth—and not a bit rotted, either."

"Good enough," Aunt Maura said. "We've got a good batch of summer herbs, along with some seed saved from those special pink tomatoes."

I jumped up and was outside the door before they had set down their cups. Ditsky's old brown pack, which seemed too big for his thin back and bony shoulders, was resting in the sun and soaking up the heat. I thought I could smell the smells of all the places he had walked.

He hunkered down beside the pack and began to unfasten the many straps that held it together. Some had buckles and others were buttoned or tied. There were pockets sewn on the sides and a big one across the back, all of them bulging. He pulled the top flap back, and as he did, he looked up and his eyes flashed.

"Fine merchandise, m'ladies," he said. His voice had the peddler's flourish I knew that he used on all the people he met along his path. It made me laugh to hear it, and Aunt Maura smiled.

He lifted out his goods, all packed carefully. Sewing things, screws and eyebolts, braided cord, knives, dye materials, small tin pots, a blue ceramic dish, medicinals, little cunning wooden toys, spices, a set of nesting boxes, paintbrushes. Some things he had on nearly every trip, like needles, and others he picked up as the fancy took him or the trade allowed. At the bottom of the pack he had folds of cloth that he pulled out one by one and spread on the frost-burned grass.

Aunt Maura started to handle the materials, weighing the heaviness of a fold of dark brown woolen on her palm.

"One more thing, especially brought from the far north where the snow has come already," he said solemnly. "Found for a princess, a gown!"

He reached way, way down in his pack and pulled out something crumpled, like a moth's wings coming from the cocoon, something gauzy and lavender, a dress, that floated on the air. He stood and shook it out.

"Oh! For me?"

"The only girl between here and the south-lands that this particular gown will fit."

I took it in my hands. It was soft, with pale purple flowers scattered across the lavender background. I pressed my face into it, and it smelled sweet and warm.

Ditsky was smiling. "I wish you'd try it on, anyway, Princess, to make sure it's right."

Aunt Maura looked up.

"What's the use in that thing, Ditsky?"

"For pretty," he said.

I held it against my worn shirt and pants, and turned twice around. "Please, Aunt Maura, we've got plenty in trade. It's so pretty."

"Go try it on," he urged.

I ran to the house and pulled off my clothes,

put on the longest cotton undershirt I had, and lifted the dress over my head. It floated down like a cloud or a feather, settled against my skin. It fit perfectly, rounding over my hips and the hem coming at my knees. The cotton underneath it was bulky. I pressed out the wrinkles in it and the dress the best I could, then walked out on the porch.

They stood down on the grass and looked up at me. I could see that in Ditsky's eyes I really looked like a princess, that I looked pretty, even with the cotton underneath and my hair all wild from being in the woods.

"Okay?" I said. He nodded.

I went back in and changed, then laid the dress carefully across my arm and went back out.

"How much do you want for it?" I asked, knowing that he would not be asking much.

"Neena," Aunt Maura said. "I think you've got more use for a piece of woolen, at this time of year. You can sew up a new jacket."

"No! He brought it special! I mean, I know I need warm clothes, but isn't there enough to get this, too?"

"Daneen," she warned.

Her mouth was closed tight, thin and hard, and I knew it wouldn't do any good to argue. She didn't want me to have the dress, that was all.

Ditsky stood between us, looking confused, and hurt, too.

I touched the ends of the sleeves where they closed with little purple buttons. I ran my

fingers across the cloth, which was silky and
fine. Then I set it down by Ditsky's pack and
picked up the piece of brown woolen.

I don't really know why I did it, but I threw
the woolen piece as far as I could. It was so
heavy that it didn't even unfold as it fell in a
dirty-colored heap on the grass. And I looked at
Ditsky, feeling tears coming up in my eyes, and
then I ran.

"Daneen! Daneen!" I heard her calling after
me, but I kept running, down to the run and to
the springhouse. I went inside, where it was
cold and wet and dark. I closed the door tight
after me.

*We were many days away from Hagerstown. We
were in the mountains. My feet hurt from walking,
but the man called Ditsky couldn't carry me because he had a heavy pack, so we walked together
slowly on the old road under the trees.*

*He had given me one of the bracelets he wore, a
copper circle, and I held it in my hands and
turned it around and around. The sunlight flashed
off it, red, where the beams came through the
trees.*

*The forest was around us, the trees tangled to-
gether by vines and all the smaller plants that grew
up. They didn't look at all like the trees in the park.
Some had broken branches, or were dead. Where
the pavement was broken on the road, small trees
had started growing.*

"Come on, Princess," he said.

I hadn't wanted to go with this man, but Mom

told me I had to go. I wondered how long it would take us to walk to this place where Aunt Maura was, in West Virginia, and how long it would be before she got there, too.

He motioned for me to speed up, and so I slipped the bracelet over my arm and started walking faster. He took his walking stick in his other hand and put his hand down for me to hold on to. I pushed the bracelet up so that it hung on my elbow, and I held his thumb.

"When are we going to stop?"

"At the road fork there's a friend, Walter, and if we walk fast enough we may make it to his house by dark. But not before the rain, I think."

I looked up at the sky that showed between the trees. There were clouds covering all the sky except where the sun was going down. I could see the clouds moving, faster than the little wind there was down on the ground.

We walked. We went off the road to go around a pile of wrecked cars, on a faint path that went in a half circle through the woods. When we came back out to the road, there were two men standing by the rusted cars, watching us.

Ditsky stopped at the edge of the woods. "Good day," he said.

The men didn't answer. Both of them were bearded and dressed in dark blue uniforms, like policemen and not soldiers, but they didn't wear any badges. They were much taller than Ditsky. One of them held a gun in his hands, and the other one had a gun on a sling over his shoulder.

"If there's something you're watching here, we'll be on our way," he said.

"Where to?" asked the one with the gun on his shoulder.

"Down the road."

"Your girl?"

"A friend's." He squeezed my hand, then let it go. The one who was talking leaned toward the other man, and they spoke low together.

"A child's a lot of care on the road. You want to get rid of her?"

"No."

"Peddler," said the second man, "everything you got's for sale. How much you want for the girl?"

Ditsky changed his grip on the walking stick. "I've got a pack full of trade goods," he said, "but she's not for sale."

"We don't want your trash, peddler. The girl'ld be worth something, trained up right. Or maybe that's what you got her for?"

He didn't move. Standing beside him, I could see him breathing deeply.

The first man unslung his gun. "Two rifles against your stick, peddler. Do you think that's good odds?"

"No."

"We'll pay for her, in gold."

"Or we'll take her," the second man said.

I wanted to run, but the trees closed around behind us, and I knew I wouldn't ever find my way out.

"Men," Ditsky said at last, as though it was something he had thought out. "I don't know what your loyalties are now. You've got some, even if just to each other. My loyalties are to the mother of this little girl, who asked me to take her out of

*the cholera at Hagerstown to safety. And I'll do
that."*

"Or die trying?" the first man said.

"Or that."

*The first man stood for a little time with the gun
in his hands, then he slung it back on his
shoulder. He made a hand motion to the second
man. "I'll say this for you, peddler, you're no coward. I hope you make it to wherever you're going.
You and the girl."*

*Ditsky put his hand up in a sort of salute. Then
he took hold of my hand, and we walked away
from the wrecked cars and the two men.*

*The dark came around us and the rain started.
Ditsky helped me put my coat on and set his big
hat on my head, then he pulled a piece of plastic
over his shoulders and we kept walking. The rain
bounced loudly off the plastic, and it ran off the
brim of the hat in front of my eyes.*

*We came to the road fork and a tall white house
that was dark in every window.*

*We went up on the porch. Ditsky pushed open
the door.*

*The house was empty. The furniture still stood
in all the rooms, but the friend Walter was gone.
The house was damp and cold.*

I sat and watched the water flow through the
long strings of moss and algae in the springhouse. Light seeped in around the eaves and fell
across the rounds of cheese on the stone shelves
and on the milk can cooling in the stream.

I put my cupped hands in the flow and

splashed water on my face, washing away the tears.

Someone was coming. I rubbed my face dry on my sleeve. The door opened and Uncle Ted stood there, outlined by the sunlight.

"Hello."

"Hello."

"I heard that you and your aunt had a falling out."

I wiped a stray bit of water from my cheek. "Ditsky brought me a dress. She wouldn't let me have it."

He came in and shut the door behind him. The loose overcoat he wore smelled of smoke. He sat down beside me and stared into the water.

"What are you thinking?"

I shook my head. The way I felt about Aunt Maura now wouldn't bear telling.

We sat there and watched the water bubble and slide through its stone channel. A cardinal whistled from a limb near the springhouse, "bird-y, bird-y, bird-y," a winter song.

"Neena," he said.

"Um."

"I caught up with Ditsky-the-Peddler, down the road. He said he had something for you."

I felt a little stab of anger, again.

He reached inside his coat and pulled out the dress. "Here," he said, and as I reached out my arms he draped it across my wrists, a cool purple cloud that melted into the dampness on my skin.

"How did you get it?"

"One of Maura's butcher knives."

I tried not to smile, knowing how much store she put in those knives, but happy at what he had done even so. I buried my face in the cloth and felt flushed and flesh-warm with the gift.

"You'd look just like a girl used to, if you'd wear that."

"I know," I said, softly, to the water. "Like a princess."

Chapter Eight

——◆——

IT WAS ONE of those days where the sky hangs gray, not raining or snowing, but reminding you that it is fall and that snow or rain are waiting.

The sun had come up in a thin slice of red, a gap in the clouds to the east and south. The sky closed up not long after sunrise, a heavy, slow gathering of clouds. Even the smoke from the chimney hung like wool. The time went on from morning to noon to afternoon with not much change in the gray light.

I'd worked around the house with Aunt Maura all day, washing dishes and clothes. The clothes hung on the line between the maple trees now, just as heavy as the clouds and dark with the water in them.

We had split kindling and brought in kindling and wood and coal, coal that Aunt Maura had found and dug from an exposed seam in a ravine, which we crossed at its narrow upper end when we went to gather herbs on the ridge. The pieces of coal could be chunked out of the hillside like thick slabs of slate. They were dull black, shiny where they had broken free of the seam, and sometimes on their flat surfaces were the fossils of ferns and plant stems. Coal piled on top of the wood made a long, warm fire through the night.

It was dinner time. I stood at the sink, peeling potatoes into a pan of water and watching the night come. The leafless trees were pressed against the dark sky, like the fossils.

Uncle Ted came walking up through the woods from his still. His red hat bobbed among the limbs and dead leaves like a cardinal bird.

He came into the yard and stopped at the well to draw up some water and rinse the dirt from his hands. He saw me watching in the window and he put up his hand, the water dripping. He wiped his hands off on his pants and came in, stomping his feet on the stone step to knock off the mud.

"What's for dinner?"

"Potato soup."

"Okay. Where's Maura?"

"In the herb room."

He went in to the front room and sat in his chair by the stove, stretching his legs out straight and leaning far back. He picked up the book I had started reading, *Tess of the D'Urber-villes*, one he had brought back after being down in Middletown to see Matheney about changes to some metalwork he'd done. I don't know if he bartered for it or found it in one of the aban-doned houses along his way, but it had black spots of mildew on the bottoms of the pages. The binding, which was brown leather-like with gold lettering, had been chewed by mice. I was only as far as the second chapter in the first part, where it talked about the village of Mar-lott.

Aunt Maura came out of the herb room. She shut the door carefully behind her, so as not to bother any of the smaller herbs where they lay drying on screens.

She sat down in the big chair and rested her head against the back.

"Tired, Sis?"

"Just worn out," she answered. "I'm glad to see winter coming, for the rest."

After a moment, she laughed.

"Maura Lee?"

"Remembering winter. That long slope behind the house that ended in the open lot by the Browskeys?"

"The one we used to slide on?"

"Remember how we used to go all night? Snow down our backs and just as wet and cold, bruised from flying off the inner tubes on the jump, but we never wanted to stop."

"Until old Gregor came out and yelled at us."

Aunt Maura's smile faded. "That poor old man."

They stopped talking and just sat. Uncle Ted had put a green log in the fire, and it hissed and flared.

I sprinkled just a little bit of black pepper on the soup. We were nearly to the bottom of the can. I wondered where the pepper had come from—certainly not from peppergrass, nor the green peppers we grew in the garden.

"Soup's ready," I said.

They got up, came to the kitchen, and sat down in their regular places at the table. I ladled out the soup into the bowls and set the kettle on the side to keep warm.

We finished one bowl. I brought seconds.

"I'm going to run the whiskey off this week, tomorrow maybe, if it clears," Uncle Ted announced.

"Matheney get the problem with the cap taken care of?"

"I think."

"It's about time that you're getting that meal used up. I've been worried about mice."

"Couldn't run it until the still was ready and we had the barrels made."

"True enough." Aunt Maura ran a crust of bread around the inside of her bowl to take up the last of the soup.

I had been to see the still as it was being built, the firebox made out of slabs of stone, then Matheney's copper pot with the arm running out of the top to the coil and the cooling box at the stream. As I understood it, the liquor came out hot, as steam, and then it cooled to a liquid in the loops of coil and in the water-chilled box.

There were piles of wood for firing, charcoal for filtering. New barrels were lined up by the barn, ready to be moved, along with the boxes of glass jars. We helped with the hauling, but the distilling was Uncle Ted's work, like the herb gathering was Aunt Maura's and mine. We knew about whiskey-making from the asking, not the doing.

I set the dishes in the sink, under the faucet that hadn't given water for years. I took the kettle from the stove and poured hot water over them to soak while I finished clearing.

"What's this book?" I heard Aunt Maura say.

"Something I picked up for Neena."

The book slammed down on the table. "Garbage," she said. I winced at the sound in her voice.

"What's wrong with Thomas Hardy?" Uncle Ted was tired, but just warm enough and full enough from dinner to feel up to a fight.

"Nothing more than the rest. She hasn't done a thing but read novels since you got her started. Romantic trash."

"You'd rather she didn't read?"

"Not things that will be of no value to her."

He laughed. "I'm sure the history of a dead nation will be of great service in handling oxen. Or maybe she can learn to hold off a raiding band by reciting the periodic table."

"Things won't always be like this."

Uncle Ted leaned forward. "You don't think? You don't think that once people start tearing at each other, they get that blood taste, like a dog or a wolf, blood on the tongue? The rebellion against Washington that became a war between the Coastal Cities and the Sutherland, that didn't end there. The whole continent is infected. We've been quarantined."

"Order will come back. Someday."

"Why? Because we were civilized? Were the United States? We're not anymore—we're tribespeople. Clans. Middletowners against the outside. The Dauchertys against the world."

"You think you know." Aunt Maura held her hands clenched between her knees.

"I've seen."

"You've seen some things, not everything, not everywhere."

He grinned, a naked kind of grin.

She stood up, walked to the window, and stood there with her face close to the glass and her own reflection. I could tell by the set of her shoulders that she was trying to get hold of her anger.

Uncle Ted picked up the book and began to leaf through it, the pages falling softly against each other.

"I'll tell you something, Ted," she said, turning around and standing with her hands pressed back against the windowsill. "Daneen was entrusted to me, to raise her and educate her, and I'm trying my best to do right by her and by Terra."

He kept watching the pages as they riffled past his thumb.

"Damn it, Ted, listen to me!"

He looked up, startled.

"You come here and turn everything upside down. All your big ideas. This liquor thing, that had us hoeing corn all summer long, my herb gathering neglected. And this—these books . . ."

"You don't want me to teach her?"

"Oh—" She glanced toward the kitchen, and I pretended that I was washing the dishes. "I just don't think what you're teaching her is appropriate."

"Maybe it's the teacher you really object to. Me. Men in books. Men in general."

"That's not true."

"Men who come in here and upset everything that's quiet and orderly."

"Yes, orderly!" she shouted. "We were doing fine, Daneen and me. We had enough to eat, we were warm and safe. She was learning to do something useful, take care of herself."

"Is that kind of independence important?"

"Yes."

"Then Neena should have shot when she had me in the sights of that rifle," he said.

A chill ran over me.

It was quiet in the front room. I slopped the water up over the dishes to make a sound, something to break that awful silence in the house.

"I'm sorry," she said. "I didn't mean that you weren't wanted here."

"I can finish off that whiskey, for my part, and

I can be down the road." His voice was stiff, proud and angry.

Everything was splintering, again. Somewhere in me someone cried, remembering people leaving, people lost. I remembered a single moment, when my mother stood in the sun and her hair glowed. I remembered her pale face on the pillow, sick, her hair spread around her like a halo. Then a candle taken away, then darkness.

"Ted."

I turned around. Aunt Maura stood in the middle of the room. She held her hands at her sides, open, looking strangely useless without some work for them to do. Uncle Ted sat forward in his chair, his face turned up and lighted strangely from below by the red fire showing through the stove door.

"You're all the family I've got. And Neena." She whispered, an anxious sound like I'd never heard from her.

"Kinship." He threw the word down like a broken stick.

"You're not my kin, you're my brother. You can't let words come between us. Nothing can come between us—nothing."

Uncle Ted put his head down. He closed the book and set it on the floor by his chair. Then he stood up and he looked sideways at me, then back at Aunt Maura.

"Hey, Maura Lee." I heard him walk across the room. "You think I'd leave you now?"

Chapter Nine

———

THE WHOLE BOX was bad, a good pound of the root of Great Solomon's Seal. I could tell as soon as I turned over the roots and saw the white powdery spots of fungus and the black mildew on them.

I remembered the day we had dug them, close and hot, and then a storm that night, and after that a week of rain. Nothing had dried right. We thought these were dry enough to store, but we had been wrong. Aunt Maura would be upset. She'd rather a whole bundle of herbs were lost than roots, because there was so much more work to the digging and cleaning and drying of roots.

I took the box of damaged root over and dumped it in the discard barrel, along with the other herbs and roots which couldn't be sold. There was mullein flower, faded from age, and shepherd's purse, which was infested with some kind of small insect larva.

Great Solomon's Seal, polygonatum multi-florum, I remembered to myself, looking down at the knobby roots. The many-kneed.

The names of the plants ran through my mind, the long Latin names that had been the names of healing before the great civilization and now, again. And each of the names attached to flowers, or fruit, or the look of the plant in the fall with withered leaves.

The names were a code, some of which I knew.

Sanguinaria, blood, for bloodroot. Eupatorium perfoliatum, the foliage of boneset, which was run through by the stem. Geranium maculatum, for the spotted leaves of cranesbill. Panax which was allheal, Panax quinquefolius, the name of ginseng five-leaved. Words from old, dead tongues, pieces of the code, the secret of the names of the plants we harvested.

Secrets. Uncle Ted had his own, a language that he spoke to himself.

I turned over the black-stemmed fronds of maidenhair, set them back in their tray, and laid the thin cloth loosely over the top.

When he first came to us, he carried his secrets like a rash on the body, visible, with the scar on his head and the way he had of watching and watching. Now, the secrets were inside, carried like an illness. Every illness breaks out sooner or later in a sweat or a chill.

The night after he chased the thief, he came back with blood on his sleeve. He was quiet all the evening. Late in the night he woke us with his screaming about the Change, the Change and dying. Horrible, horrible screams. Like ones I remembered sometimes from myself a long time ago.

Most times I couldn't remember the time before I was with Aunt Maura, as if everything I'd lived until then was behind a wall of river fog. Then the fog would open up and everything was clear, sharp, all the lines and shadows.

I pulled another of the trays from its slides in the tall dry-herb cabinet. Bindweed, the heart-shaped leaves shriveled on the thin trailing stems. There wasn't much there. There were other purgatives, more popular.

I wondered what Uncle Ted was hiding.

I wondered why he spent nights beside the fire, rolling tobacco in carefully cut squares of paper, smoking the precious cigarettes slowly, staring at the light patterns on the floor.

Lots of people were made quiet by what they'd seen in the war. The black Sumblins had a grown son who never spoke, who didn't feed himself or dress himself, but sat on the stoop of their big brick house which Aunt Maura said used to be the senator's house. His quiet was like that of someone stunned and just now waking up, or someone clenched in a fever.

Uncle Ted's quiet was more like someone who has made a promise, half known, half secret, like the knights who made vows of a year and a day in the Arthurian tales.

Sometimes I really thought of him as a knight. He brought me books and odd things he found in wandering the old roads and going into houses. He would give them to me, smiling, his eyes bright blue and open, but he never opened all his thoughts to me.

He had gotten me the dress that Ditsky brought, though Aunt Maura had taken it away and folded it up in the top of her closet. Once when she was away I took it down and smoothed it out and touched the cuffs and the collar, and the hem caught up with neat long machine stitches. Then I wondered what it was like, before, when women still wore flowered dresses in the great cities of NordAmer. Then I wonder how men and women were.

Uncle Ted had whispered to me that men and women lay together for their happiness, with the ones they chose. There doesn't seem to be much choice now, with people scattered so far on the land.

A shiver came over me, and I realized that I was still holding that tray of bindweed, tilted now so that some of the leaves were near to dropping from the edge.

I righted the tray. The leaves were brown, and I rolled one between my fingers and it went to dust. I dumped the tray.

The scent of the discarded herbs went up with the dust and hung in the air, catching the light that came in through the north window and swirling among the bundles of plants hanging from the ceiling beams. It smelled something like an overgrown field in the spring, when the sun warms all the dead grasses and plants that have been under snow.

I was waiting, waiting. I was like seeds under snow, waiting like roots and frozen seeds under snow for something to happen.

The thought of snow made me shiver again and I pulled my sweater together and buttoned it, then felt the chimney where it backed onto the herb room from the kitchen. It was warm to my hand. I moved up against it and stood, getting warm.

The Johnsongrass on the field outside the window blazed in the sudden light of the sun through clouds. It was red gold. It was the color of Uncle Ted's beard.

He was as handsome as any of the men I had read about in the books he brought. He was safe and comfortable because he was kin, but at the same time a stranger, mysterious.

I wondered if I had absorbed some love dust, working with the herbs, one that only this summer had had an effect. An aphrodisiac. A lot of the medicinals were supposed to have that property, including ginseng.

But Aunt Maura never seemed to be bothered by any wanting. She went day to day the same. At night, she lay in her bed, straight, her hands folded over her ribs—I watched her breathing as I lay awake—while I watched the thin moonlight and starlight spread across the floor.

I don't think I had ever heard her say to her brother that she loved him. Not in that many words. I had said I loved him, many times, first as a child and then, at least I felt, as a woman. Sometimes I felt caught between, and I was not sure how it was that I loved him.

I felt the warm of the chimney bricks on my shoulders and legs. I thought about Uncle Ted, his white teeth and the way his blue eyes turned smoky sometimes when he sat with me and we read. His big hand turning the old, fragile pages. His hands that worked. Hands that had fought, too, and been bloody.

Tears started in my eyes and I wiped them away, but then I was crying, and ashamed to be crying, alone and secret, alone in the room.

Chapter Ten

————◆————

THERE WAS SNOW on the ground, a dry snow, fallen in the cold of the night and already beginning to soften, slide off, and melt in the sun. It covered the clumps of grass and clung to the crotches of the trees, on the old bird nests and squirrel nests. It left bare the circle of ground under the pine trees and on the sheltered side of rocks. The trunks of trees and fence posts were very black against this first whiteness; things moving on the land were very dark, sticklike.

I saw the man coming over the ridge, a black movement among the stiff, black trees.

"Aunt Maura," I said, going close to her. The day was still and voices carried. "Someone on the ridge."

She rested her load of wood farther back in the crook of her arm and bent backward to balance it, shaded her eyes with her free hand, and watched.

"Coming from the barterman's way," she said. Then, after a minute of watching him walk, "I believe it's him. Now whatever could bring him out of his place?"

Uncle Ted came toward us from the house. "What is it?"

"Someone coming," I said.

"The barterman," she added.

He stared at the ridge and the figure of the man, now bigger and bulkier, moving down it.

"Come on." He took hold of my arm and started to pull me toward the house. "Let your aunt handle this."

I looked back over my shoulder. Aunt Maura didn't make any sign. I went with him, pulled by his insistence as much as by his hand.

"Stay in the house," he said as we reached the stone stoop.

I wanted to ask him why, what there was to fear from this man whom Aunt Maura dealt with, but his hand was hard on my arm like the grip of fear and I didn't ask. I went in, and he closed the door, hard.

I went to the sink and leaned against the counter, watching. Aunt Maura had put down her load of wood and was waiting. Uncle Ted went and stood beside her. The barterman was at the edge of the woods, coming into the fields.

Uncle Ted didn't act like other people did when the barterman was mentioned. Most people stiffened, avoided looking at you, talked about other things. It was as if they were embarrassed, and somehow afraid of being Changed, too, by talking about it. But Uncle Ted—there was something else, not other people's kind of discomfort or dread or outright fear. Something else.

He turned toward the house and I ducked.

After a moment, I eased up the window about an inch, so that I could listen.

"Morning," Aunt Maura said. I heard a low murmur in return, in a deep voice which was not Uncle Ted's. I couldn't pick out any words.

"You've come a good walk."

More of the deep, whispering voice, strange, that made me shiver to hear it.

"Where have they been seen?"

The barterman again.

"Where do you get this information?" Uncle Ted cut in. "We haven't heard anything about raiders in the area."

The answer. I strained to make words out of the murmur.

"You came here to warn us?" Uncle Ted replied, sounding suspicious. "You deal with these people, don't you? Isn't it to your advantage that you barter the things they steal?"

There was a long silence. I lifted my head up above the windowsill.

Aunt Maura was facing me, and facing the barterman, who had his back to the house. Uncle Ted stood between them.

The barterman was bigger than Uncle Ted, only a little taller but a lot heavier through the body, his shoulders massive, like the trunk of an oak. I remembered the stories, that he had cut and hauled and raised the logs for his cabin all by himself. He wore a brown, plaid coat and a black, knitted cap pulled down to his ears. All that I really could see of him, of his flesh, was the hands, which hung from his coat sleeves, broad as cut slabs from the same oak tree.

"I think you owe my neighbor an apology," Aunt Maura said.

"It's true, isn't it?"

One word from the hulking figure of the barterman, whispered, but I knew somehow that he had answered, "No."

I watched Uncle Ted's hands. They moved, as if by themselves. The barterman's were still.

"My brother's had some bad experiences in the Coastal Cities," she said, trying to make peace between them. "The things he's seen... You have to understand that."

I heard the barterman answer. I heard Uncle Ted, angry, cry out to cover and deny the whisper.

There were bodies beside the road. From a long distance away, they looked like piles of stones, or dirty snow the way it once was pushed up against the street curb by the plows.

I walked closer. I saw the clothes, then the people in the clothes. They were new dead.

They did not look like victims of the same disease, but like different creatures, thrown together.

Most of the faces were hidden, but the naked hands that covered them were strange, too. The hands of the adults were soft and pale, swollen looking. The children's hands were shriveled up, the bones showing through the dry scales of the skin and the little nails hard and thick and yellow at the ends of the fingers. All the arms and hands looked like they were holding together, holding tight; they all might have fallen there in a heap, like people playing on the grass and rolling over and over.

It was very quiet. I stood in the path and watched a few flies buzzing over the pile. The bodies had not begun to smell much.

One face showed at the edge of the heap. All the hair was gone, not just on top of the head like most older men, but even the eyebrows. The face was heavy, a broad nose and a heavy chin, and ears that seemed to be too big. I looked at that face. The eyes were closed behind red, puffy lids, and I wondered what color they had been.

Then I saw the soft, pink collar where it rested against the throat, and the flower-shaped cluster of pearls.

It was a woman, Changed even more than the others, not a woman anymore. Not a man. Something else.

I had seen other bodies, of people who died from disease and were taken care of and buried by friends. A lot of people died. Those faces, even after fevers, looked peaceful, looked forward to the Heaven-lands. These faces only looked inside, at the clawing of the Change.

I felt my hands on the cold ledge of the sink. I shook my head, shook away the bodies and the faint smell of summer rot.

The barterman still stood with his back to me,

but now Aunt Maura stood facing Uncle Ted, between the men, separating them. Uncle Ted's face was red and his fists were clenched and straight down at his side. The wind pushed his hair back and the scar showed white on his forehead. I had never seen him look like that, angry and scared at once.

"What's between the two of you has to stop," she said. "We haven't got the luxury of hating our neighbors."

The barterman's voice was low, like before, and even. He talked for a little bit, and then he held out his hand, that huge hand, and I saw now in the open sun that his skin was yellow, a strange not-human color, like that of a flower or a leaf—the weird print of the Change on his body.

Uncle Ted stumbled back a step. The barterman said something.

"You're not alive!" Uncle Ted screamed. "You're dead, back in the cities, dead on the streets, dead like the rest of them. Nothing lived after the metachemicals. Nothing, not you, not you and your watching and your interfering. You're dead bones!"

The barterman's hand went back to his side. He nodded to Aunt Maura, and then he turned away from Uncle Ted and began to walk back in his tracks to the ridge and his place on the other side.

Aunt Maura went to the barn.

Uncle Ted walked toward the house, his head down. His shoulders were stiff and his hands were clenched. I stood in the window and watched him. When he was almost to the house he looked up and saw me, but he didn't see me, because his face was twisted and his eyes were seeing bodies and rotting things like the ones I remembered, too, from a long time ago.

Chapter Eleven

HEIDI MOVED IN her stall. Her hoofs rustled in the straw, hit hollowly against the door. Sunny or the calf, disturbed, thumped against the side of its stall.

A warm current of cattle smell moved through the gaps in the boards. It was a smell that was safe, a smell of regularity and of care taken. There was the same kind of ordinariness in the sound of the cattle breathing and the sound of their stomachs working.

We were the ones who were breaking the order of things.

We waited, sitting on an overturned hay crib, hidden in the unused stall where we could watch, through the vertical spaces between the siding boards, the house and the pathway up from the road. Aunt Maura held the Winchester, loaded, resting in her hands. Uncle Ted, who was between us, had a revolver.

The barterman had warned Aunt Maura that raiders had been seen camped on White Oak Ridge, seen by one of the scavengers who brought him barter. A band of ten or a dozen, he said, not counting the smallest children, who wouldn't be trusted with weapons. They didn't have any cattle with them, so they were moving rapidly. Their backtrail led to the Line—it looked like they were headed south and east. We were directly in their path, if that was so, and this was the very night most likely for them to arrive.

If the raiders came, then they would find an empty house, not much to take but half of a dried-apple pie on the counter, bread, and some staples. Clothes, a few. The best of the herbs were bagged and hidden in the hayloft above us. The whiskey was buried in the safest place of all—two storage barrels rolled into a hole dug in and under the manure pile, then covered.

The raiders might take what they could find and leave. They often did, especially if they were in a hurry to get south, or were afraid of being chased. We wouldn't bother them, then. It was best not to be looking after trouble. But if they tried to burn the house or barn, or take the cows, then they'd find a battle.

It was cold, sitting there in the dark, the cold of a closed place that settles in your bones.

More clouds had moved in after the clear morning, and now the sky was half blue-dark and half filled with the clouds that blew from west to east across the quarter moon. The stars showed bright between the clouds.

The moonlight reflected from the snow that had not melted, and from the windows of the house, and the dented metal patches on the roof. The path was a cut of pure darkness against the snow-spotted ground.

Heidi put her nose against the side of the stall and breathed out, then in, and the white of her breath showed for a moment against the light seeping in between the boards.

"When?" asked Uncle Ted.

I didn't need to see Aunt Maura shrug.

"They generally follow the roads," she said, low, "knowing they'll find houses. But I'm worried they might come overland, straight from Middletown, if they move through there."

"If they're coming at all."

"I'm going over on the other side. Keep a good watch, here." She lifted the rifle in both hands and stood, awkwardly, and went out of the stall and quietly across the barn floor to the other side.

Uncle Ted brushed the hay chaff and dust from a board and laid the revolver there. He put his hands behind his head and stretched.

"Cold?"

"A little," I said.

"Come here."

He unbuttoned his big coat, and I sat on his lap and he folded me inside the coat. The heat of his body went around me like a blanket warmed by the fire. He tucked the coat as far around me as he could, then rested his gloved hands on my

knees. He put his head to one side so that he
could watch; his beard scratched my ear.

"Better?"

"Uh-huh."

I nestled back into his chest. I felt safe, raiders
or not, safe in the strength of his arms.

He lifted one hand and untangled a strand of
my hair from his beard, then smoothed my hair.
The tips of his fingers brushed against my
cheek, very gently, then again, and again.

He put his hands around my waist and pulled
me close against him. I felt a hardness against
my body, pressing against my seat.

I trembled.

"You aren't cold now, are you, Neena?" he
said, his voice as soft as the stroking of his hand
had been.

I sat still. His man's hardness moved against
me. I felt in myself a kind of answering movement, an unfamiliar warmth between my legs,
and an ache in my breasts.

This is how it is between animals, I thought.
Between people, too, the heat and the hot
breath. My mind tried to think of why it was not
the same for people. There was more, gentle
love, like in the books, but the pressure between
us said no and the weak warm trembling in my
muscles also said no.

I looked at the white moonlight outside and it
seemed impossibly cold there, empty and lonely.
And there we were, warm, closed in together,
and the dark of the barn folded around us like
another covering between us and the cold white
sky.

He moved against me, and without thinking I moved back, against him.

I thought about his room, upstairs, and his bed, which was right against the wall under the one small window that looked east. About him alone, lying there, looking at the hills which went on and on to the east. And him alone, lying there, screaming into the night.

His breath rushed past my ear. I was surprised to hear my own breath, and it faster, too.

"Anything, Ted?"

I jumped at Aunt Maura's voice, a whisper carried from the other side of the barn.

He breathed in, then answered, "No."

The cold came in against me, as it must have against Uncle Ted, because his hardness was gone and his breathing was slower and lighter again.

He pushed me forward and I stood up, went and sat down beside him. He buttoned his coat again and picked up the revolver and rested it on his knee.

"More I think about the lay of the land, more I believe they won't be coming overland. This band doesn't know the ridges hereabouts, from what the barterman said he heard." Aunt Maura came into the stall and sat down beside me.

I shivered, one spasm.

"Why, you're about frozen," she said. "Put that collar up on your coat."

I put the collar up and rested my face down between the open ends, warming my chin.

The cold crept up from the floor, through my

feet and up my legs. I felt like I was sinking slowly into water, half-frozen, a slushy winter pond, but inside me a coal of warmth burned still. I shivered between the inner heat and the outer cold, and was stretched thin between them like a piece of white sycamore bark, to be flamed to ash or frozen and shattered.

I wished we could have stayed in the house. I wished even that the barterman hadn't come across the ridge to warn us and made us spend the long night, anxious and waiting and bone-chilled.

I hugged my arms around me and tucked my hands under my arms, then I leaned against the wall that separated our stall from Heidi's. The barterman—I wondered what his face looked like, if it was human or something else. Aunt Maura had never told me.

I must have fallen asleep, then, because the very next thing was morning, a pale winter sun slanting through the boards.

I looked up and there was a face peering down at me, shadowed black, and the gleam of eyes. I pulled away.

"Neena." It was Uncle Ted. "We're going in. The danger's past."

I stood up and, when he wasn't looking, I watched his face. I wanted to see where that stranger had come from in the first light. Or maybe that face had been just the end of some other dream.

Chapter Twelve

◆

KINGSTREE RUN, WHERE the Hollises lived, was tucked in between its ridges like something precious. It was flat, rich land spreading out on each side of the creek, pastures, and fields, easy to the tilling. The hillsides, brown with the oak trees that still kept their leaves, came down steeply to the bottom.

The land was named after a great sycamore tree that had stood by the run, Aunt Maura said, one so big that the first settlers camped inside its hollow trunk until they built their cabin. They were the McClungs. Later, the Carters had moved in and spread their family up and down the run.

The great tree was later struck by lightning and burned. The McClungs had died out, and the Carters were gone now, too. The farmlands were overgrown with the brier thickets of wild white rose and blackberry, now bare except for dried-up berries and red rosehips. The Hollises lived on the last of the old Carter farms, right up at the end of the hollow.

The road that led along Kingstree Run was kept open by the comings and goings to the Hollis place. It was worse this fall than it had been last year at this time. The paved surface was torn into ragged blocks by the plants that had rooted in it and grown, grasses and then woody plants, and finally, sapling trees. The pathway wandered from side to side of the roadway, avoiding the worst heaves and the trees. At one place it made a big loop around a new widening of the creek, which was hedged with a thick growth of willows and sycamores and box elder.

I sat in the back of the cart, holding on to the side and trying not to get my teeth knocked out when a wheel bottomed into a hole.

Aunt Maura clucked to Heidi and turned her to the left. Sunny responded to the movement and pulled left also.

A muskrat sat in an opening among the willows, close to the water and its mud-stick lodge. Its little front paws worked, turning over a piece of dripping weed, while water slid from the brown hump of its back.

Whump! The right-hand tire dropped off the hard surface into a rut, dry but hard with the frost. I hung on as the wheel slowly rolled up and out.

"I think you should complain to the road commission," Uncle Ted said.

Aunt Maura smiled, just a little, but she kept her eyes straight ahead, as if she were driving an auto-car instead of the cart, which was the bed of an old pickup truck, cut free and set up to harness the slow power of the oxen. Aunt Maura and Uncle Ted sat on a little rough bench, and I rode back in the ridged bed.

We generally went to the Hollises two or three times a year, and always in the late fall, when the day was clear and cool, for the butchering. The first fine day after what was Thanksgiving.

I watched the weaving of willow branches as we rode past, slower than we could have walked.

I liked seeing old Mr. Hollis. He had a thick head of white hair, a beard just as thick, and a face webbed with wrinkles from years and years in the sun. If the work went well, butchering or cider-pressing or bean-shelling, he would sometimes get out an accordion and squeeze tunes from its yellowed keys and dusty bellows. His three daughters, all grown, were more somber than Aunt Maura, if that was possible. They all three had straight, light brown hair, eyes the same flat color, and though tall, they stooped forward and stood with their arms crossed as if to hide their small breasts.

I had never seen Mrs. Hollis, who'd been dead for many years, but I imagined the daughters took after her.

Lisa, Ella, and Leila. Lisa, the eldest, had white in her hair and a little pot belly resting like disappointment for a child. Ella and Leila were twins, just alike in their sad faces and slow movements.

I breathed in deeply and smelled smoke.

"They've got their fire going," I said.

"Sure do," Aunt Maura said.

Uncle Ted sat, nervously cradling a rag-wrapped bundle on his lap. It was a jar of his liquor.

The cart lurched forward behind Heidi and Sunny. I shifted onto the other hip to ease the bruising.

Aunt Maura guided the cart through a mess of

frozen ruts where the road had dropped away. I could see the smoke of the scalding pot fire rising beyond the trees.

The farm came in sight, a tall two-story house faded from white, with many narrow windows; the long barn; all but the one tall fence which enclosed the barnyard rotted down and left to lay. The Hollises let their pigs forage free on the ridge, eating acorns and roots. Using dogs, they rounded them up in the fall, then butchered or bartered all but a few breeding head.

The pig pole was raised high, and a blackened, fifty-five-gallon drum steamed over the fire.

I could see the daughters moving around the yard, laying out the implements on planks laid across sawhorses, bringing knives and bone saws, and deep buckets and pans. Not a bit of the pig would be wasted, from the hocks to the head, not even the blood, which was saved for blood sausage. That last was something I couldn't eat, or maybe as Ditsky told me once, I just hadn't had the need to yet.

One of the daughters saw us and lifted a hand. Not a wave, just recognition. She dropped her hand and stared.

We drove through the yard, past the drum and the lightning-damaged cottonwood tree, then around behind the house to unyoke Heidi and Sunny and tie them each by their halters to a tree, out of sight if not smell of the blood-work.

I jumped off the end of the cart, then helped Aunt Maura carry the tub over to the butchering place.

"Hello, Lisa," she said. "Ella, Leila." We set down the tub, and she took the round of cheese from it and a gallon jar of milk. "Something for your table."

"Kind of you, Maura," one of the twins said. She headed for the kitchen, where the dinner would be laid out. The Hollises didn't bother with cattle, though they had chickens and goats as well as hogs.

"Where's your dad?"

"Down behind the barn, doing the killing."

Uncle Ted started in that direction.

He went around the barn. After a little bit, I saw him coming back, bent over as he dragged the weight of a fresh-killed hog. Behind him came Mr. Hollis and a man I didn't recognize, leaning into the rope as they dragged a second pig.

They pulled them into the yard. The first hog was hoisted, back feet first, with the pulley to the top of the pole, then with Lisa holding the pan, Mr. Hollis cut the jugular vein and the blood spurted. The steam from the hot water rose up around the body, and the fresh blood steamed. The second hog was raised up over the limb of a tree and bled the same way. The rest of us stood around in a circle, waiting.

"I'm Cliff," the strange man said, shifting from foot to foot. "Cousin to the girls."

It must have been on Mrs. Hollis's side that he was kin, because like the girls he was tall and lanky and brown-haired. I guessed that he was about twenty years old. His beard was brown and not all the way filled out, though trimmed up it mightn't look so bad.

"Where are you from?" Aunt Maura asked.

"Ohio River," he said, but nothing more. He looked back at me through the steam.

The work began. The men lowered the pig into the water to scald it, then hoisted it back up. I took the worn scraper that one of the twins offered and began to scrape the bristly, black hairs from the hide. Aunt Maura worked to one side of me and Lisa to the other. The heat in the carcass soon left, and then the wetness was cold on my hands.

It took a long time to clean the pig, scalding and scraping, then scalding again to loosen the stubborn hairs. Finally, the pig was white and clean from its ears to its tail. The men took it away and replaced it with the second, brindled-brown hog for scalding.

We added a bucket of water to the barrel and waited for it to heat.

Mr. Hollis stood back, next to Aunt Maura.

"You ought to raise a couple pigs," he said.

"I'm busy enough, Bill," she said. "I'd as soon trade you some herb tea or tonic roots for your smoked hams than raise and butcher a hog myself."

Uncle Ted went behind the cottonwood tree and brought out his jar of liquor. A little was already gone.

"Hollis?" he said, lifting the jar up. Light shone through the liquor, the color of the water in the sulphur-spring pool, deep with old leaves. He'd aged the liquor with charcoal in the barrel, and it was amber and not clear like it had first been when it came from the still.

Mr. Hollis nodded and took the jar, tipped it back, and took a short drink from the offered side of the rim. He handed it to Cliff, who sipped a little from the same spot, then handed it back. He flushed, warmed by the liquor.

Uncle Ted drank two swallows, wiped his mouth. The twins stared at him, as though they had some kind of agreement. He saw them and he smiled.

"A sip, girls?" he said. They blushed and Ella motioned the jar away. He smiled again, then went to put the jar back behind the trunk of the tree.

It was steady work from then on. I helped the twins scrape the second hog, while Aunt Maura and Leila helped the men gut and wash the first pig, saw off the head, and split the body along the spine. The intestines were set aside to be rinsed, packed in salt brine, and used later as sausage casings. Leila took the liver and heart and kidneys away, and the head to cook down for what Mr. Hollis called "head cheese."

The second hog, scraped smooth, was cleaned and halved. The four sides were hung from a horizontal limb of the cottonwood tree, red meat covered with rich cream-colored fat to be rendered down for lard.

Dinner time, and I was glad because my arms were shaking from the long work of scraping. Everyone was sweaty and greasy from working around the boiling water.

The Hollis women had the dinner set out on

the long kitchen table. There was our own cheese and milk, and the strong-smelling cheese they made from goat-milk. There was boiled sausage, freshly fried ham slices, and bowls of turnips and potatoes and mashed squash.

Mr. Hollis sat at the head of the table, with Lisa on his right hand and cousin Cliff on his left. Then the twins sat next to Lisa, and I sat next to Cliff, with Uncle Ted next to me and Aunt Maura at the foot of the table. We just sat down without any planning, yet it all seemed formal once we were in our chairs and facing across the table. The Hollises all bowed their heads for a moment before eating.

Uncle Ted had his jar in front of his plate, now about three-quarters empty. His eyes were bright blue and they gleamed in the afternoon light, which streamed down the length of the table from the kitchen window.

"The twins tell me that you're not from around here."

I turned around. Cliff was leaning toward me, waiting for an answer.

"No. I used to live in Hagerstown. And when I was real little, in Baltimore."

His eyebrows lifted in a flat arch when I said that.

"You know the cities?"

"I don't remember much," I said. In my mind I saw the flat bright blaze of the ocean, and the sails of the boats, and the gray towers of Baltimore beyond.

"More'n I've seen, though. My whole life, I been at Sistersville, never even so far away, nor east nor west, as this till now." As he talked, his hands moved, marking out roads or rivers or the sides of mountains. In the warm afternoon light, he didn't look so washed out as he had before.

"What's it like—the river?"

He sat back a little, thinking. "Well, it's broad there, and mostly the water's clear, except when there's been heavy rains. My pa said there used to be barges, strings of them, on the river before the wars, but now it's mostly local boats. The locks at New Martinsville been blasted and so you can't go north, and to the south the river isn't safe around that old DuPont plant."

"Does the water shine in the sun, so you can hardly look at it?"

"Sometimes. Sometimes it's like looking at snow, or a mirror. Other times it just is green and smooth. I go out on the river a good bit, fishing, hunting ducks."

I picked at the sausage on my plate.

"So why are you here?"

"I hadn't ever been nowhere. I told my pa that I was going to travel up and see how the Hollis end of the family was, but he knew I was just wanting to move around some." He stroked his thin beard. "I had a horse. It got stolen. Now I'm not in any hurry to go back to the river, seein' as I'll be walking."

We went back to eating. I saw that the twins, sitting across the table from us, were whispering together, their faces colored up. Sometime before dinner, each one had brushed her hair and tied it back with a bit of white lace. They kept looking at Uncle Ted.

The jar in front of his plate was empty. He was leaning forward, his face red, grinning so widely that his eyes were nearly closed.

"Do you like to go fishing?" Cliff said.

I turned back toward him. "I've never been. Are there fish in the run?"

"Just minnows and some small fish—you use those for bait. You have to go down to the river at Middletown to really catch fish."

"I don't have anything to fish with."

"That's easy enough to fix up. There's an extra rod and reel in the shed. Leila's gone with me before."

"What do you catch?"

"There's bass, and walleye-fish, and carp. They're all big fish. If you want, you can use worms and fish for crappie in the bay. They make a fine fish fry."

I wondered if the fish he named looked like the ones that I dimly remembered, laid out silver on the ice in the fish market. They were ocean fish, though. The only fish I could remember eating was some dried fish at Frederick, and it didn't taste good.

"Sometime, maybe," I said. "I'd have to ask Aunt Maura if it was all right.

"If what was all right?" asked Uncle Ted, so close that I felt his breath as he spoke.

"If I could go fishing."

He put a hand on my shoulder and turned me around. "With him?"

"I only asked her as she's a neighbor," Cliff said.

"You asked her because you're a goddamned

horny kid who wants to get her down by the
river and spread her legs."

Cliff pushed his chair back and stood up.
Uncle Ted stood up, and he pulled me up with
him and held me around the waist.

"You've got no call to be saying that," Cliff
said. His face was set.

"I'll say what I see as true," Uncle Ted answered. His hand moved back and forth on my
stomach, and his other hand was still on my
shoulder, holding me firm.

"I don't think the boy meant anything by asking," Mr. Hollis said.

Then I felt the hand move up from my stomach
and across my chest, and then it was on my
breast. The heat of it went through my shirt, and
it seemed as if his bare hand was bare against my
skin, burning my breast. I turned away from
Cliff's stare and Mr. Hollis's calm stare. I tried to
look at Aunt Maura, but I couldn't turn that far.

"Neena is in my house and she's going to stay
there," Uncle Ted growled. His hand pressed
harder. "I'm the only man who's got a claim on
her."

He pulled me around, tight against him, and he
bent forward and kissed me. His lips were hard
against mine. His mustache and beard scraped
against my face. I opened my eyes and saw the
glitter of his eyes, drink-warmed and violent.

I tried to push away from him, and I felt the
vibration of his laughter against my mouth.

His grip lessened a little and I spun away, but
his hand still kept hold of my shirt, and as I
broke free the fabric ripped and buttons

popped. The air was cold against my skin, burning like the heat of his hand had burned.

I pulled my shirt together and backed away from the table. The men stood, separated by the space which I had filled. Mr. Hollis was half out of his chair. And the Hollis women sat and stared, and Aunt Maura sat, pale and frozen. I looked at her, and I hated her for her silence.

I ran out of the kitchen and around the house, to where the oxen were tied. I fumbled at the buckle of Heidi's strap, got her free, and led her to the harness.

The wind, bitter as the winter that would come, made my fingers stiff and slow, but it didn't stop the burning of the blood which had risen to my face, nor did it lessen the heat and pain in my breast, the bruise of that hand which had held my flesh and claimed to own me.

Chapter Thirteen

———◆———

THESE WERE THE shortest days of the year.

It was the end of December, the time when the cold and the dark were hardest to bear. Even January, with its snow and wind, had longer days and some promise of spring to come. But these days the dark held.

It used to be that people would light fires on the shortest day, the solstice, to help the sun turn away from the darkness and return. They gathered in green branches of pine and holly and mistletoe to remind them of the warmth. Aunt Maura said that when the Christian faith arrived in the cold north countries, the old habits of lighting fires and candles, and gathering greens were all just included in the celebration of one Christ Child's birth. He was the Son and the Sun all together.

She gathered in green branches, and I never had asked her which it was she celebrated, the solstice or Christmas. Maybe both.

There was a long stem of holly over the door arch, between the kitchen and the front room. It was from a male tree—no berries. There was a bunch of long-needled white pine, tied with a red yarn and hung on the front door.

We sat around the stove, our faces red-lit from the glow through the mica-paned door, the only light in the room. Aunt Maura was knitting, which she could do in the dark. Uncle Ted sat right close to the fire, feeding it with sticks of oak when it died back, his face down and his eyes on the moving red light on the floor. I sat over near the frost-whitened window, watching the clouds move across the scarred quarter-face of the moon.

There was enough wind to bend the dry hay stems and weed stalks, and to make a thin whining sound at the corners of the house.

Sometimes it lifted dry snow or ice and threw it, hissing, across the crusted snow.

I think I must have fallen half-asleep, because the hissing and the whining began to move together, in rhythm, like a slow song.

I shook my head to clear away the dreamwebs, but the music remained.

I saw something moving on the old road.

"Aunt Maura," I whispered. "Look."

There was a dark line on the snow-covered road, a wavering line like a string drawn. I still thought that I was dreaming. The line jerked along, people close together, and they shuffled in time with the rattling music and the wail of their voices. The flickering light from the moon showed their pale faces, the dark holes of their mouths, and the beating of their hands on tambourines or each other's bodies.

"What in the hell is that?" said Uncle Ted.

"I'm not sure," Aunt Maura answered, her voice also hushed to a whisper.

The line came closer. The leaders started to disappear below the slope which ran down from the house to the road.

Like a piece of yarn unraveling, three of the people began to move away from the main line. They came up on the lawn. As they lifted their feet to climb up, I saw that they weren't wearing any boots or shoes.

"Harvesters, though I've never seen this. It has to be them," Aunt Maura said.

She pulled me back away from the window. Behind us, I heard the familiar sound of bullets being chambered in the Winchester. Uncle Ted held the rifle, standing back in the black dark near the bedroom door.

The three people came up to the window and stood, staring at the house. There was a woman, wrapped in a long mantle that trailed in the snow, and two men, both of them in rags, their arms bare. They were singing. They swayed to the rise and fall of the song, a chant, a wail, with voices too exhausted to sing.

> "Fallen, fallen, oh, Babylon,
> Oh, the place of demons,
> They drank the wine,
> They trampled the poor
> they turned away from the Lord's sign.
> Fallen, oh, the gilded whore."

The woman lifted her hands up to the moving clouds. The mantle slid down her arms. She was naked under the mantle, her skin as blue-cold as the moon.

> "Lord, we feel your hand.
> We have been set apart.
> We were not pleasure-takers
> in the streets of Babylon
> and we will not be weepers.
> Oh, their sins were high as heaven.
> There is no mountain high enough
> to contain their torment now,
> there is no measure of sorrow."

One of the men stepped forward. He fell to his knees in front of the window and pressed his face against the glass, melting the spangles of frost. He took his cheek away and looked with one wild eye through the crescent-shaped mark.

"The Lord walks through the world, he breaks the sinners, his feet are stained with their blood," cried the woman.

"Touch your foreheads," the man called, his strong voice strangely cracked. "Do you touch the seal of God there? You cannot feel it because it is not there. We are the plagues of God. We are the locusts who will eat up the sinners. We are the fire and the smoke and the sulphur. We will burn you with fire and drown you with waters of blood. We bring in the harvest, keeping the good ears and burning the tares on a hot fire."

"Oh, fallen, fallen!" screamed the woman.

"These are the last days. The Lord waits for all to be completed. Are your souls marked for the harvest?"

Suddenly it was very quiet. The man at the window pressed his fingers against the glass and began to mark a symbol in the frost. His fingertips slid on the glass, a straight line down from the crescent. Harvesters—it was a scythe.

The man was gone, and the woman and the other man. After a long time, when we heard only the whining of the wind in the eaves, we went to the window.

Where they had stood there were the melted marks of feet, and dark stains on the snow. Bloodstains.

"Damn," I heard Uncle Ted say.

Aunt Maura went to the stove and began to poke up the fire, rearranging the logs and then putting one more small piece on top. She swept some ashes from the fender.

"They're gone," she said. "Let's have some real light."

She lit a splinter of wood from the fire and touched it to the wick of the kerosene lamp on the kitchen table. She adjusted the wick and brought the light into the front room and set it on the low table.

"Cheer up, Neena."

I tried to smile for her. I knew she was upset by the Harvesters. We all were.

"What makes them like that?" I asked.

"Ignorance," Uncle Ted answered.

"No," said Aunt Maura. "They want to believe there's some reason for the wars and the killing. They want to have some reason for their fear that is easier to accept than that people are insane. So they make God insane."

"And not for the first time," Uncle Ted added.

"No," she said, quieter. She stared at the lamp flame, her back to the window. The light made hollows under her cheekbones and marked out the wrinkles at the corners of her eyes and the long lines to the corners of her mouth. She breathed in deeply and then, long, out.

"Well," she said, "enough about them. They're gone, good riddance."

"And it's Christmas, or close," Uncle Ted said. "Time for giving gifts and being happy."

He opened the drawer in the little table,

where we kept ammunition, and took out something. He brought it into the light. It was a present, wrapped in brown paper which had been smoothed out, and tied with a bit of the same red yarn that Aunt Maura had used to tie her greenery.

"Merry Christmas, Neena."

He laid the package on my lap.

"Open it."

I touched the yarn. It was bright against the paper. I pulled it off the package and opened the paper.

His present was a book, as I knew already from the weight and shape. Unlike other books he had brought me, this one was not burned or broken or insect-chewed. There was a crisp paper cover with a picture on the front of an old stone wall.

"The Poetry of Robert Frost," I read.

I opened it and saw the irregular lines of poetry on the stiff, white paper. Words about trees and fences and other familiar things.

"Do you like it?" His voice was a stroke, a soft craving for attention.

"Yes."

The paper lay crumpled in my lap, the red yarn tangled in its folds.

There were candles, long pale yellow tapers made of beeswax, that smelled warm and sweet as they burned. The light flickered in the room. There were many candles lit, for joy, even though other times only one would burn.

Mom sat beside me on the couch. She wore a green dress. Her red hair lay in waves on her shoulders, and when she laughed the candlelight was reflected on the strands of her hair.

She laughed often. We sat with the others, Mr. and Mrs. Leveaux and their children, Dan and Ofalia, the people who had taken us into their own home in Hagerstown. It was Christmas. There was a tree decorated with pine cones and silver tinsel and glass ornaments, with presents underneath wrapped in paper which we had decorated.

"Laura, do you know how wonderful it is to have a Christmas?" Mom said to Mrs. Leveaux.

"We don't hide it anymore, do we? Saying it's for the children."

Ofalia, who was ten, took the presents from under the tree and, reading the names out loud, handed one to each of us. Mine was wrapped in white paper decorated with red snowflakes. I held it in my lap while everybody else unwrapped theirs. The red ink which had been brushed onto the paper began to rub off onto my fingers.

Mom leaned toward me. Her hair fell against my cheek and the soft corduroy of her dress shushed against my leg.

"What are you waiting for?" she said.

The spreading circles of light became one circle, the flame lit on kerosene and smelling of oil as it burned. The memory of my mother faded, too. I waited for the memory to come back.

"I thought you'd like it."

The last spark of the memory was gone, and I

raised my head. Uncle Ted was leaning forward in his chair.

"I do like it."

"You don't seem to."

"I do. Thank you."

He sat back and the chair groaned. "Thank you," he mimicked.

"What do you want me to say?"

He stared at me, his eyes narrowed. I wanted to believe there wasn't any hate in that stare, but there was. Tangled up with the desire that I used to think was love.

"I was remembering something—about when I was with my Mom."

"Well, it's good you have such wonderful memories, because Terra Daucherty is dead."

"Ted!" Aunt Maura cried out.

"The day Neena figures that out for herself is the day she'll be free of all this remembering crap. There's nothing to remember, nothing but bones."

I heard Aunt Maura arguing, but the words weren't clear anymore. I sat in my chair, stiff and silent. It was the first time anyone had said that right out, not caring.

I closed my eyes, but the tears ran out anyway, and when I opened them the room swam with light. His beard flamed red, a blotch of color like my mother's hair. His voice rose against Aunt Maura's.

"Damn you both and damn this Christmas. Go on, run after the Harvesters if you want to celebrate something. They know what there is to celebrate."

He pushed out of his chair and walked across the room, his boots hard against the floor. He climbed the stairs to his loft.

Aunt Maura sat in her chair and I sat in mine, a million miles away. The lamplight and the firelight were reflected on the black window and shattered among the frost.

Chapter Fourteen

———•———

THE PROBLEM WAS that the black thread blended into the dark blue of the sock. I had taken down the lamp from its nail and lighted it, but the day had gone out since then, and the window behind me was dark. I bent over my mending and followed the silver point of the needle in and out of the fabric, binding the hole that had opened in the toe.

"You'll be blind in a year, working like that," said Uncle Ted.

"I can see."

I heard him get up from his chair by the stove and walk into the dark part of the room. He brought back the lantern we used for going to the barn, swung it up, and set it in the middle of the table. Straw and dust settled from the base. The bail handle rapped against the glass.

He lit a twist of paper in the stove and touched it to the wick. A warm, yellow light spread out, past the edges of the table, spilling over. I frowned at those ragged stitches I had made.

"I wouldn't want those blue eyes of yours all squinted up before you're sixteen," he said.

Aunt Maura stomped her feet on the porch. The door creaked as she shouldered it open, a rush of cold air and frost coming in before her. She dropped the wood in the crate by the stove.

"Why've you got that lantern out, Daneen?" She was out of breath from carrying the big load, but she was angry, sure enough.

"The poor girl couldn't see what she was doing with that one light you let her have."

She turned to Uncle Ted.

"We can't waste fuel over the darning of a few socks. You could've let her sit by there, where she'd get some better light."

Uncle Ted leaned back on the kitchen chair until it creaked and balanced on the back legs.

Aunt Maura reached across me and turned the wick down. The little flame disappeared down the slit with the wick and went out, seeming to take all the room's warmth with it.

The front legs of the chair came down with a thump. "You want her blind? You'd think you're the one providing here."

"We can't afford to waste it."

"I want Neena to have the light." He fisted up the hand that rested on his knee. "Remember, sister, I'm the one who made the liquor that's buying that kerosene."

Aunt Maura got stiff, the way she does. She went back outside. There were little clear puddles on the worn kitchen floor where the snow had dropped off her boots and melted.

Uncle Ted opened his fist, slowly, and patted his knee. "C'mon, Neena, leave that be. You can do mending in the morning."

I kept on darning the toe of the sock, but I saw when he took the little bag from his shirt pocket and carefully rolled and lit a cigarette. He flicked the burning end of paper into the open door of the stove.

"Hey, Neena."

I knew I'd better get some of that pile done before dinner. There was nothing I liked less than mending.

"I got this for you."

There was a paper sound, and I looked up. Uncle Ted had a little book, smaller than his hand, without any covers.

"A peace offering," he said.

It was the second book he had brought me since Christmas.

He smiled, open, welcoming but almost a little afraid.

Of all things to mend, I liked socks the least. I dropped the sock and the darning egg and needle on the table, and went over.

It was a thin book, smaller than his hand. There was a burned place at the top of the first few pages, and smudges of soot. Probably taken out of some burned-out house. I reached for it, but Uncle Ted pulled the book back and tucked it inside the open front of his shirt.

"You know, I like poetry, too, Neena. I would like it if you would read something to me, like you used to." He patted his knee again.

It was warm next to the stove. I sat down on his knee.

Uncle Ted put his arm around my shoulders. He tried to squeeze me close, but I sat straight up and just reached inside his shirt for the book. He let me take it.

The pages were stuck together. When I turned them, the burned edges broke off and fell.

The book fell open in three or four places. At one, there was a drawing of a bird and a vine, and the name "Rubaiyat," strange and distant.

> *"Come, fill the Cup, and in the fire of Spring*
> *Your Winter-garment of Repentance fling:*
> *The Bird of Time has but a little way*
> *To flutter—and the Bird...."*

"Daneen!"

I hadn't heard Aunt Maura come in. I slid off his lap like snow off the barn roof.

Aunt Maura threw down the kindling. Splinters and pieces of wood flew across the bare floor.

She didn't say anything. She was too angry. I bent down and began to pick up the scattered kindling.

"Get dinner on the table." I nodded, keeping

my eyes safely down, hidden by my hair. "Ted, help me get things ready."

She went out, slamming the door behind her. It bounced away from the latch and shut again. Uncle Ted chuckled and slid his hand down my back and over my rear as he went after her. I pulled away, without even thinking, my mind still on the poems in the little book, which he had put back in his shirt.

I set out the plates and the cups, and made coffee. The beans were ready, warm at the back of the cookstove. I stirred up the cornbread and put it in to bake.

When everything was ready, I looked out the kitchen window toward the barn, but there was no sign of them coming back. Just two sets of tracks which disappeared into the long shadows cast by the moon. It was a day past full. I pulled on my coat and went out.

There was no light at the front of the barn, where the cattle were, which meant they were still back below the hayloft. I walked around the barn, making new tracks beside theirs.

"...half a Harvester yourself, Maura Lee."

"That's not true, Ted. I wouldn't be hauling this to the barterman if it was."

"Oh, some of your morals are easier than theirs. You don't think the liquor I make is the devil's own water of damnation—don't dare, considering. But still, you've got a lot of the psalm-singer in you."

I ducked under the shafts of the wagon and sat down on a bag of salt. It wouldn't do to interrupt them until they'd finished their talk.

"But they're right about some things."

"About the end of the world?" Uncle Ted's eyebrows lifted and his blue eyes shone. "About roaming the countryside, setting their snares, breaking into people's homes, looking for sin? Or what they think is sin? Killing folks down in the Circle of Salvation at Penitence, killing them to save their immortal souls?"

"No. Of course not."

Aunt Maura was working on the drawband for the sledge, which was loaded and covered with a stiff canvas, tied down. You could barely see the roundness of the glass jars full of corn liquor that were our barter. This was the last of the whiskey that Uncle Ted had made, not a very big load, but it was valuable as the ammunition it was barter for.

Her face looked thinner because of the shadows from the lamp, which hung from a hook on a beam. Uncle Ted stood facing her, with his hands on his hips and the light full on his face.

"You can't do it forever."

"Do what?" Aunt Maura spoke out hard, and her breath made a little cloud.

"She's no child. And she's got a pretty face," he said, then added low, "the worse for her."

"And what do you propose I do, Ted?"

I sat back farther under the wagon, even though I was sure the light didn't reach.

Uncle Ted spread out his hands. "Like I said, you're acting half a Harvester. Our own mother wasn't any man's bound wife, nor was Terra.

Fourteen is a woman, old enough to know her mind."

"The wars ended a lot, a lot of that kind of choice. Neena—she needs to be taken care of."

"If it's that you want, then you should know she'll be taken care of by one man you know. I'm blood to her, Maura."

She dropped the drawband. "I won't have it."

"You won't have it?"

"She is your *niece*."

"Don't argue eugenics with me, Maura. Every ruling house in those old European histories you treasure relied on alliances made with blood kin, as close, or even closer. You needn't be personally concerned about the fate of the American gene pool."

"There are other choices."

"Are there? It isn't just my need, you know. There's her need, too. Or have you forgotten?"

She glared up at him, looking almost a match for Uncle Ted, though he was a head taller.

"Why don't you leave it up to Neena? Why don't you ask her, right now?" he said.

I didn't move. They couldn't see me.

"Is she in here?"

"She's under the wagon." He dropped his hands off his hips and began swinging them back and forth, back and forth. The ragged sleeves of his plaid hunting coat pulled up and showed his wrists, and the red hairs on his arms.

"Come out, Daneen."

I reddened right down to my fingertips. I

crawled out and brushed the cobwebs out of my hair.

"How long have you been listening?"

"Dinner's ready. I came out to tell you dinner is ready. I haven't been here very long. I didn't want to interrupt."

Uncle Ted brought his hands together, thump, at the front of the swing. The sound made Aunt Maura draw back.

"We've been talking about you, Neena," he said, tilting his head back and looking down at me. His lips were curled up just a little, the beginning of a smile. "Your aunt and I."

"Leave be, Ted." I didn't have to look over at her to tell that she had gone stiff. Uncle Ted's eyes lost that laughing color and turned dark and sulky. "Go on—we'll be right in."

Maybe it was because Aunt Maura had never had any children of her own that when I crossed over from being a child she hadn't changed her way with me, I thought, walking back through the snow to the house. She treated me the same now as when I had been a little girl, not asking me what I thought or what I felt.

There had been times when I wanted to go up the stairs to Uncle Ted's loft and lie with him, as he had said men and women did. He had touched me in ways that made my heart beat like a hammer in my chest. And then there had been times, more and more lately, when he was mean and dark-faced, so that I feared the weight of his hand on me.

He'd never used a light in his loft. The one

window faced east toward the ridges, and beyond them the coast and the empty cities and the sea. His bed was set right under that window, even in the bitter weather. No matter how I felt, I thought that most likely I would be looking out at the ridges and toward the sea soon enough. Aunt Maura might say no for a time, but I had never seen her stand fast against Uncle Ted. He was her brother.

And, too, I was old enough now to know that running would take me no place safe.

I knocked the snow off my boots against the outside wall. The kitchen seemed summer-hot after being out in the barn. I took off my coat and hat and gloves. I set the beanpot on the trivet in the middle of the table. Right after, I heard Aunt Maura and Uncle Ted in the entry-way. They must have said what they wanted, because there wasn't any talk as they came in and washed up for supper.

We ate. The cornbread had dried out for waiting. Aunt Maura ate fast and not very much.

She put her fork down, click clink, in the middle of her plate.

"You won't go with me, Ted?"

He looked up from the cornbread he was buttering. Then he looked back down, took the slice, and bit off the end.

"Ted?"

"Stop it." He pushed back from the table and put his hands on his knees. "I'm not going, Maura. Tonight, nor any night."

He left his place and went back to the chair

by the stove. He rolled and lit another cigarette. Some of the precious tobacco sifted out
of his fingers, fell to the slate, and mixed in
with the ashes and splinters and pieces of bark.

"Won't let me forget," he muttered. Then,
louder, "What was done had to be done."

"Get dressed, Daneen."

I whirled around so fast that I nearly upset
the lamp on the table, made it flicker and burn
a black tongue of soot onto the side of the chimney.

"You want me to get dressed for outside,
again?"

"That's what I said." Aunt Maura's mouth was
set. The words came out flat, as though they'd
been squeezed between her lips.

"Why?"

"You're going with me. To see the barterman."

I felt my blood pound, with excitement and,
too, with relief that I'd not be alone with Uncle
Ted.

I'd been as far as the ridge, and looked down
on the old meadows growing up now in sassafras and dogwood, to the corner of the barterman's property. Now I would be able to walk
out of the trees and through the meadows. Then
I remembered to myself, if I could have forgotten for even a second, the massiveness of his
hands when he'd stood in our yard. A war
Change.

I heard it said, once, between Aunt Maura
and Ditsky when they didn't know I had
heard, that Uncle Ted might have worked in
the places where the metachemicals that

brought the Change were made. The Change, which went down inside the skin, into the cells, and made bones grow again, and made skin and hair turn color. It made young people old, and old ones soft like children. Then it killed them.

I don't know. He never told me that.

I looked sideways at him. The cigarette he held in his hand, unsmoked, had burned away to a long ash, and as I watched the ash fell and rolled down his pant leg to the floor.

I went and got my boots, and sat down at the kitchen table to lace them up.

"Why are you taking her, Maura?" His voice seemed to echo from far away.

"It's time she learned to deal with him. In case I'm sick, or hurt."

"There's no need for her to see that." He turned on me and grabbed my wrist, brought his face up close to mine. His breath smelled of ashes and smoke. "The barterman's uglier than anything you've ever seen, Neena. He's a freak, something that should have died in the city."

"What's outside the man can't be helped, Daneen. The barterman has been Changed, that's true, but he's a fair man, no raider or wanderer. I imagine that he's a good man, from what I know of him. As good as anyone can be now and live."

He let go so suddenly that I lost the end of the bootlace I'd had in my hand.

"You've never feared to leave her with me before."

"She'll go with me."

He got up and went to her, and took her shoulders in his hands. "If you're feeling that you don't want to go alone, tonight, I'll go. As far as the fence corner. I won't go to the grove."

She ducked out from under his hands, and came and stood behind the chair where I sat.

"What if the Harvesters are out on the hills tonight?"

"She can shoot."

"Maura!"

I couldn't help but look up. His hands hung down at his sides, and his face was so white that the scar on his forehead stood out. I felt sorry then for Uncle Ted, because he was strong and fine-looking but twisted up inside, too, angry but also afraid and not able to do much about either one.

I tugged the knot tight on my bootlace and went with Aunt Maura, out to get our coats and then to the barn.

I helped her get the sledge out of the barn. It was hard pulling, the waxed metal runners squealing on the wooden floor until we hit the snow and the weight eased. We came around by the house.

Uncle Ted was standing in front of the open door with no coat on. The light from inside and the moonlight cast two shadows from him. He held the Winchester in his bare hands.

I went and took it from him. There were five rounds in the magazine, one in the chamber. I made sure the safety was on.

Uncle Ted held out extra bullets. When I took

them, he held my wrist, between the mitten and the cuff of my coat.

His hand stayed clenched on my wrist for a long, warm time.

Aunt Maura had the sledge poised at the gate, facing north. When she saw me come running, she threw her weight against the drawband. The sledge creaked and then slid smoothly.

Chapter Fifteen

———◆———

THE GROUND WENT out from under Aunt Maura's boots, the white snow falling, hollow, blue-black as a shadow. She dropped straight down. Branches broke and snow came up in a cloud, which hung for a moment and then filtered back into the hole.

The sledge tilted, tilted, I started to reach for it and it slid and went down.

There was a sound of things breaking, wood and glass. Aunt Maura moaned.

I went down on my hands and knees, and crawled toward the jagged hole.

"Aunt Maura?"

"Stay back, Neena!" The words were cut off by the effort of her breath. She was breathing in short puffs, huh huh huh. I could hear that, though I couldn't see her.

"Are you hurt?"

"Stay back!" I squatted back on my heels. There was a sharp, bitter smell of spilled liquor.

"Neena..."

"Yes."

"The Harvesters...made this...I think. Sledge is on my hips. Too steep."

I didn't want her to talk any more.

"I'll go for Uncle Ted."

Huh huh huh. "No. Barterman."

"But I can't! Not without you! I can't go to the barterman alone!"

"Just a man, Neena. Go."

She panted like an animal in a trap. Like a cow that had gone down in the stall and panted herself to death trying to drop twin calves.

The cold seeped down into my boots. Her feet were cold, too, pinned, the fiery cold liquor running on her skin.

"Go."

"I'm going. I'll leave the Winchester." I made sure the safety was on and pushed the stock over the edge. She grunted, reaching. I was holding the very end of the barrel when I felt her take hold. I heard her flick off the safety.

"Go."

The ridge path was hardly to be seen, but I followed it by the faint shadow thrown across the snow-covered trail by the moon, and by seeing where the tall, dead grasses marked each side of the beaten way.

The snow had drifted. In places it was deeper than my knees; in others it was hard and ice-crusted, a handbreadth deep.

I tried to concentrate on the path so that I wouldn't stray off it and lose time. I tried to stop seeing Uncle Ted's half-smile, shadowed by the lantern light, to stop seeing the triumph in his eyes.

I counted my steps, lost track, started again. At last I was at the top of the hill above the grove.

There was no light from the barterman's house, hidden in the pines, but I knew that he was there.

I could feel my feet getting white and frozen from standing. I curled my toes against the hard soles of my boots until I felt them tingling.

"He's just a man." Aunt Maura said that, trying to help. Just a man.

The old fence line ran straight down the slope in front of me and into the pines. The rotten wire sagged between the posts, which leaned toward the east, away from the snow piled up by the wind. But there wasn't any wind. The tall white pines, which even in the smallest breeze sigh and sigh, stood quiet in their own shadows at the foot of the hill.

I walked along the old fence, down to the pines. Once I was in the grove, I could see a shape darker than the trees, dark right to the snow, and a thin gleam of yellow light at the edge of a shuttered window.

The barterman's house was made out of logs, white pine logs that he had cut and notched and dragged and lifted up into a house, all by himself, people said. The logs were striped pale and dark, peeled wood and bark, the spaces between them chinked up with what looked like mud. Snow clung to the upper edges of the logs.

I tried to pull the mitten off my right hand, but my fingers were stiff cold. I used my teeth. I banged on the door, on the rough gray planks.

There wasn't a sound inside the house.

I knocked again, harder, felt the cold sting of feeling coming back in my hand. There was a whisper of sound, like a cat walking across the floor.

"Barterman." My voice was shadow stiff, quiet as wind in pine branches. "Barterman, Barterman." Louder. "It's Neena, Neena Daucherty, Maura's niece."

The cat sound again. The latch lifted and the door swung in.

"Barterman?"

The room was nearly dark, just an edge of light spilling from the side, candlelight.

"Where's Maura?" A strange, whispery, low voice.

"She's trapped. She's in a pit, under the sledge, where the path is narrow." Suddenly I was out of breath. I swallowed to get it back. "She fell into the pit. She said the Harvesters made it."

Light flared, bright yellow light from a lamp, making me blink.

The barterman came around the door, following the light.

He had a face like the broken stones of a cliff sometimes make a face against the sky— all heavy and overbalanced. The brow bones and chin jutted strangely out, and the eyes were just dark places, like caves under the stone. His skin was yellow, slick-smooth where there should have been hair and brows and beard.

He held the lamp higher, and his eyes kindled. They were gray-green, like melting ice in the spring.

I shuddered, hoping he took it for cold. It was as though a stone or a tree, one I had seen every day, had woken up to stare at me with new and curious eyes.

"So you're the girl. Come in, Neena."

I stood there on the stone stoop, feeling colder for the warmth which spread out from the open door.

"You've got to help her."

"Of course. Come in."

I moved one foot, the other one followed. The barterman closed the door. He set the lamp on a table, by the candle which showed its light through the window. There was a book, open, on the table. He reached for it.

"Please hurry, please, Barterman."

His hand was knobby, overgrown, resting on the thin book like the root of a tree thrown up on the bank by a flood. The fingerbones had grown again, like the bones in his face, when the Change took him. I closed my eyes. Even for Aunt Maura, down in the shadow in the snow, I couldn't do anything else.

"Am I only Barterman to you all?" He asked it softly, not really as a question needing an answer. "Only Barterman?"

I opened my eyes and stared at the hand on the book.

"I don't know any other name, any name but that one."

"My name is Arden. Call me that."

"Arden. Is that your given name?"

"It is my name, the name I give myself. From the country where I grew up." His lips were soft, without anger, in that stony face. "Arden, on the river. Where the laurel comes down to the water, and the water runs in a hundred streams among gray stones."

"Mr. Arden, hurry. Please."

His hand moved across the open book. "Yes." He went into another room, taking the lamp and leaving me with the candle and the book.

The table was smooth and polished, a light-grained wood, maple, maybe. It reflected the flame and the dull gold edge on the pages of the book, a book without any torn places or burns. I wondered what it was he was reading, but I didn't dare to move it.

I looked away, at the shadows on the wall. The wall was covered with books, all colors of bindings and all sizes, some of them scorched or black with mildew and others clean. I shivered just as though I'd fallen in a snowbank.

His steps came first and then he came in, carrying a coil of rope and a heavy bow saw with a red handle. He had a pistol in a worn holster on his hip, a long knife in a sheath, and a black wool knitted cap pulled down to his eyes.

"Let's go, Neena."

My fingers and toes, which had begun to warm up, felt the cold worse when we went out into the snow. Some little clouds, which had been down on the south horizon at sunset, had blown away and the night was clear as glass and cold.

We followed my tracks. I put the toes of my rubber boots where the heels had been.

"What you said. About that place Arden, about the river," I whispered, afraid of the silence between us, walking.

"Yes."

"It sounded like poetry."

"Do you like poetry?" He didn't whisper, but his voice was low and had a raspy sound like a whisper. I realized that it, too, was the Change.

> *"The moon above the eastern wood*
> *Shone at its full; the hill-range stood*
> *Transfigured in the silver flood,*
> *Its blown snows flashing cold and keen,*
> *Dead white, save where some sharp ravine*
> *Took shadow, or the sombre green*
> *Of hemlocks turned to pitchy black*
> *Against the whiteness at their back.*
> *For such a world and such a night*
> *Most fitting that unwarming light,*
> *Which only seemed where'er it fell*
> *To make the coldness visible."*

* * *

He made a short motion with his hand, which seemed to cover all the woods and fields.

"'Did you make that poem?"

"No, no." He laughed, a hoarse, uneven sound. "That is just a piece of a poem, an old poem called 'Snow-Bound.' By a man named Whittier."

I looked more carefully, trying to see things as that man Whittier had, and not just as meadows and oak trees with their leaves gone or clinging two or three to rattle. "Cold" and "keen" were words you'd use to describe a knife, but they were right. They were poetry.

"The last class I taught was on Whittier."

I waited.

"Don't you want to know where I come from, Daneen Daucherty?" He turned to me, and the moonlight polished his smooth yellow skin and shone on his naked brows and on his chin, bare as a woman's. "Don't you want to know who the man was before the Change?"

"It's not polite to ask questions of people that they don't want to answer. Mayn't want to answer."

It was a long time before he said anything. When he did, he spoke even lower than before, so that I could hardly hear the words over the crunching of the snow and my own breathing.

"That day we were doing Whittier, and I took time not allowed in the curriculum. We were doing 'The Grave By the Lake.'"

He stopped walking. I stopped a little way ahead, half wanting to hear what he had to say, knowing that we had to hurry.

"But you don't know about survey courses, curriculum, associate professors of American literature," he said, his voice sad and not angry at all. "You only know poetry—handsome words out of old books. And that's far more than most. I'll give Ted that, for teaching you to love those old words."

He began walking again.

"It was September eighteenth, midmorning, when they hit the city. They attacked Washington. Washington! It used to be the capital of all this, you know, NordAmer, one ocean to the other, and far as the Arctic. That was before the regions split, one from another. Then Washington was only the capital for the Coastal Cities, and only for a time.

"Five old jets came in from the north. They had markings from the Sutherland. They dropped metachemicals among all those white marble monuments. We saw from the windows, the bombs exploding high over the city and the gray mist spreading, settling. And we just put down our books on the desks and went away. It was too late, then, to run."

"Is it still there? Washington?"

"The buildings are there, clean and untouched. But not the people—they Changed, and they died. The very few resistant ones, like me, fled away, scarred. And now the white Washington buildings are empty. 'Deepest of all mysteries, and the saddest, silence is.'"

His voice went down on the last words and then stopped.

I almost cried, to hear my own heartsickness

told in someone else's words. He remembered like I remembered, and he was sad with the same things.

"I lived in Baltimore," I started, then felt the weight of that time long ago. "My mother and I—we left. We got out of the war. We went to Hagerstown."

He listened.

"She sent me here when the cholera came." I looked at my feet sinking into the crusted snow. "I don't think she's still alive, but I don't know for sure."

"That is the worst, not knowing."

"Yes. Did you have family in Washington?"

"No. Not there, not here. My parents died just before the hostilities, in a car crash."

"Do you miss Washington?"

"The city, or the people? Yes. Both. Even now." He smiled very carefully at me. "We are all missing things now, we who had them to lose."

"But you don't Change anymore?"

"No, girl. Not bodily. But there are other changes, you know."

We came to the top of the little rise and saw the pit where Aunt Maura was, a black ragged hole, flat as a shadow.

"There."

I started ahead, out of the trees, but he pulled me back. He looked carefully around at the hills.

At last we started down, the snow crunching under our boots, louder as we moved more rapidly, chasing our black shadows under the moon.

"Aunt Maura! I brought him."

She said something, weakly. I wished that I had been faster.

The barterman—Arden—tied the rope to a young, straight tree beside the path and leaned against it, then began to back down over the edge of the pit. The snow and frozen ground crumbled under his weight and then held. There was a breaking sound when he reached the bottom and slackened the rope.

Wood squealed, and almost immediately the warm, bitter smell of the liquor rose.

Aunt Maura came up, supported by Arden's arms. She was holding on to the rope with one hand, the other hanging useless. I caught hold of her and hauled her out, flat on the ground. Her face was white, marked by a black line across her jaw where a cut had welled blood.

"Take this."

The dark-wood stock of the Winchester appeared. I grabbed it. I held it in my arms, and when I bent down my breath made mist and frost on the blued steel.

He came up, hand over hand, easily.

"The sledge went straight in. There are quite a few broken jars, I'm afraid, but not much damage to the sledge," he told Aunt Maura, who was sitting under a tree massaging her legs. "I can get it out."

He untied the rope and pulled up all the slack, so the rope was bent around the tree like a rope in a pulley. The canvas and cold wood groaned down under the snow. He leaned into the rope, and the bark of the tree shredded and showed green wood. The sledge came up, tilted, rested on the edge. It fell forward and slid to a stop against the tree.

The ropes had loosened and the load shifted. He pulled back the stiff canvas and pushed aside the broken jars with the back of his heavy hand. Then he laid the canvas back, making a hollow place on the sledge.

"Get on."

"No. I can walk." Aunt Maura stood up, holding on to the trunk of the tree, swaying as though there was a wind which hit her but not the sapling.

"We'll go faster."

She climbed on, favoring her one arm, and braced herself against the sides. He stepped into the drawband. The sledge swung around in a quarter circle and began to move up the hill.

I turned around in a slow circle, the Winchester easy in my arms, checking the path behind. The shadows were very deep and black, and longer as the moon moved down the sky toward morning. But the moon moves slowly, and on the far ridge, among the young oak trees and the scrub, something else moved.

"Arden."

The creak and hiss of his pulling stopped.

I thumbed the safety off.

His shadow crossed mine. "No."

"Why not?"

He watched the ridge for a time. "We don't know who it is. That's enough reason."

We moved back behind the sledge, where Aunt Maura rested on the snow, sheltered.

The shadow didn't move again for a long time. It might have been the shadow of a tree; it was the outline of a man who was standing very still at the edge of a stand of scrub trees.

It moved again, at last, the shadow following the line of trees down toward the ravine.

"Is it a Harvester?"

"No."

"Not alone. No," echoed Aunt Maura.

The man walked slowly. He was watching the sledge. I wished that I had shot him before Arden said no. Or shot at him.

The man moved easily on the snow, not getting caught against limbs or on the greenbrier vines hidden under the snow. I wondered how much he could see of us, and whether he had a gun.

The cover thinned near the bottom of the far slope. He had to cross that. He stepped into the open space and walked swiftly across, not running. The moon lighted up his blond hair, worn long, and his beard.

"It's Ted," Aunt Maura said while I was still trying to make the words come.

"Why is he following you?"

"We had a disagreement. He didn't want Neena to come."

I glanced over at them. The barterman was looking back at me, over Aunt Maura's head.

"Let him know who we are."

"Uncle Ted!"

He stopped short, at the base of the ravine, dead still.

"Uncle Ted! It's Neena."

"Are you all right? Who's with you? Where's Maura Lee?"

Out of the corner of my eye I saw Arden smile, stiffly.

"She's been hurt, but she's here. With me and, ah—the barterman—Mr. Arden."

We got up from the snow and walked out into the open, Aunt Maura leaning against Arden and limping. We were beside the pit when Uncle Ted reached it.

"What happened?"

"Harvesters, I'd say. They dug this pit and covered it with branches. Right where you can't go to either side of the path. It's been there for a while, waiting for someone to use this path. With the snow, and all—you couldn't see a thing." She pointed down, into the hole which was so naked that it looked as if it never could have caught anything, much less Aunt Maura. "The sledge came after and pinned me. Neena went for the barterman."

"She went there alone?" Uncle Ted talked as though Arden wasn't standing right there beside me. "You let her go there?"

"They've made those who survived the Change into scare stories for children, Ted," Arden said, slowly. "You're no child. But I understand your fear."

Uncle Ted tilted his head back and stared,

not at Arden, but beyond him. "What do you know?"

"Of fear? A great deal, once. Of yours, all I know is that I remind you of things you would rather forget. Would rather have left on the beaches, in the dead cities, out of sight."

Arden looked at him straight, but Uncle Ted didn't look back at him.

"It's not fear, really, is it, Ted? It's guilt. Well, I don't hold my Change against you, not even knowing what you had to do with the wars. You were just one then, one among many, and maybe you thought what you were doing was right at the time. But I will neither forgive nor forget that time I saw you kill with your own hands."

"We were going on," Aunt Maura broke in, her voice shaking, "to finish the barter."

There was a space in which no one said anything.

"Half the barter's gone," said Uncle Ted. His voice steadied at the end.

Arden looked at Aunt Maura, then at Uncle Ted. He shrugged. "In any case, this valley is no place to stand, and she needs to get inside."

I saw her eyes turn up, white, before she started to slide, before Arden could feel her weight shift. Aunt Maura settled to the snow like a cut pine branch.

Uncle Ted ran around the pit and took her by the arm. But Arden gathered her up, ignoring him, and carried her up the hill. He laid her carefully back on the hollow place on the sledge, but the canvas was stiff and she slid. Both of them tried to steady her. Arden brushed against Uncle Ted.

He jumped away, toward the back of the sledge. "Don't touch me." He was hunched over, breathing hard.

Arden finished settling Aunt Maura, and stood straight. He was taller than Uncle Ted.

"You're acting a fool, Ted, more the fool for being who you are. The Change only mars those it touches directly, only their skin, only their bones. You know that. You *know* that." He pulled off the cap which shadowed his massive face. He didn't look at me, but I felt that he was speaking to me, or for me.

"We are the lepers of this time," he rasped. "We are feared and hated, we who suffer every day with the living memory of the wars. But I know what the metachemicals are. They will not hurt any beyond me, not those around me, not even any children I might father. I can live and have hope because I know that this pain will end with me, with the others that survived."

Uncle Ted moved closer to the sledge.

"I remember being otherwise, and there are times I wake up and regret....But I would rather be this, live inside this body, than to sleep your sleep or be haunted by your ghosts."

Uncle Ted went suddenly pale. I could see the scar on his forehead clearly. He reached down and threw back the canvas, grabbed a broken jar by the bottom.

He lunged toward Arden, reaching, slashing clumsily toward his throat. Arden put up his arm and took the shard-edge of the glass on his hand.

Uncle Ted moved back. Arden followed. He grasped the hand with the broken jar and he squeezed.

Blood dripped down the overgrown knuckles and splashed onto the trampled snow. Uncle Ted sank down to his knees, his face twisting. I heard the crack of bone breaking and the shattering of glass.

"Ah," he gasped, and he held up his other hand, fingers spread, and then let it fall to his side.

Arden released him. He stood back. Uncle Ted opened his hand and the broken glass fell. Three shards of glass hung from the torn palm and then dropped, with blood on the edges, sinking into the snow.

The sky was bright with the moon still up and the first part of the dawn gray in the east. The blood began to show red where it had been black. Light was coming in the east, over the ocean and the empty cities.

Uncle Ted got to his feet. He shook his hand and drops of blood flew, spattering.

"Come here, Neena," he said.

I looked at him and I saw someone who was kin, who wore the same eyes as my mother and myself, but who was as distant from all of us as a stranger on the hard road.

It was as if I had been under an enchantment in one of those tales of Arthur, and was just now waking up and seeing that the knight was instead someone ugly and evil and twisted, someone treacherous and cold, who had used words out of books and my own loneliness to keep me a prisoner.

I walked up in the smooth place left by the sledge, to go to Aunt Maura, but he moved and caught me around the waist and pulled me hard against him with his unhurt hand.

"I'm taking her home. Her and Maura." He put his hand against my stomach, caressing the front of my coat, the hated brown woolen cloth. His beard tangled in my hair. "Come on, Neena."

I didn't want him to touch me. I slipped away and went behind the sledge. Aunt Maura was beginning to come around.

He stepped into the drawband and brought it up tight with his weight thrust forward. He seemed small beside Arden, who waited quietly to one side with the black wool cap hanging from one knotted hand and blood seaming the other one. Arden the barterman, the Change, the poetry-reader.

If I went home, back to my own place, then I knew that soon I would be going up the stairs to the loft. I thought of Uncle Ted touching my breasts, touching me, and I saw his hand covered with blood, black blood and new red blood.

The words welled up, stronger than any fear. "I can't."

Aunt Maura lifted herself up on her elbows.

"Come on." Uncle Ted pulled the sledge around viciously and Aunt Maura was thrown backward on the remaining load. I heard another jar break.

"No. I can't go with you. I heard you in the barn—and before. All the times before." I felt the tears start up hot and I hated my eyes, eyes that were blue like his and not patient brown like Aunt Maura's, for doing that to me. "Aunt Maura, please. I can't do what he wants. I've got to want something."

"And what do you want, Daneen?" said Aunt Maura.

I blinked and looked at her. The tears made the snow and her face break into colors, move.

"I'm going with Arden."

No one said anything. Then there were footsteps. I looked up.

"Do you know what you are saying?" His voice was low and sad.

I nodded, numbly feeling the tears crawling down my face.

"It's not only poetry, you know," he said. "If you came with me, to live with a Change, a man that other people fear and hate, it wouldn't be just fine words and sentiments."

"I know. I don't know, really. Please," I pleaded. I couldn't tell if his sadness was from rejecting, or accepting. "I don't have anywhere to go. I won't go back with him."

"Maura, you can't let her." Uncle Ted's voice was shaking.

I looked at Aunt Maura, and she didn't make a sign.

I was colder in the pit of my stomach than my feet have ever been. Arden's face was bent down, and for a moment it looked like that stony cliff that I saw first. Then he turned, and his eyes were clear green and gentle.

I turned to Aunt Maura. "You said he is a good man."

"I'm a man, Neena, good and bad."

Aunt Maura nodded.

I gave her the Winchester. She rested it beside her and held out her arms. I knelt down in the snow and she cuddled me the way I wished she had when I was still that little girl. "If you're sure, Neena, if you're sure," she whispered.

I hugged her once more, hard, and I went back to Arden. We walked up the slope, following our footsteps, mine made twice. I didn't look back.

PART II

Chapter Sixteen

———◆———

EVERY HOUSE HAS a different smell.

Here, it was the scent of raw wood from the walls, wood smoke and burning candlewick (smells so familiar it was almost like they weren't there), and the dry dust smell of old paper in books. It was a smell like silence was to the ear.

It was not unpleasant, just different. Something that I had to change to meet. Something that was changed because I was here, now.

He sat across from me at the table with a book opened in front of him. The circle of light from a candle fell halfway across the pages, widening as a movement of air made the flame leap up. It was so quiet that I could hear his breathing, hear my own blood flowing. When he turned the pages it sounded like a fire starting in the room, far louder than the flames muffled inside the iron walls of the cookstove, which also provided the heat for the cabin.

I got up and set my book on the seat of my chair. He looked up, his eyes dark, set between the massiveness of his brows and cheekbones.

"I think the stew is done," I said. "Are you ready for some dinner?"

He smiled. All the people he was, Barterman and Arden and Change, flowed across his face, those and others that I did not recognize.

"Sure."

I took the lid off the dutch oven and stirred the stew, which had been simmering there for the afternoon and the early dark of the evening. There were joints of rabbit, a lean old buck that I had snared in a brushy corner of the fencerow, along with potatoes and carrots from the root cellar, and the limp lengths of beans that had been strung and dried in front of some farmer's fire.

I ladled it up into bowls and brought them steaming to the table.

Arden set out spoons and knives from the sideboard, and a loaf of bread on a plate.

He ate slowly. He ate as though he were thinking about something else and had to be careful not to make a mistake with fork or spoon. I wondered if he used to read while eating, alone.

"It's very good," he said.

"Thank you."

"I never asked you if you liked to cook. You just started doing it."

"I do like to cook. And you have so much else to do."

"Maybe you just don't want to test my camp cooking. I can burn meat beautifully. And biscuits," he said, making a motion of throwing something against the wall, "like rocks."

He looked so serious that I laughed.

"You don't believe me?"

"I don't know," I said, trying not to start laughing again. "It can't be that bad."

He smiled. "Oh, yes. It can."

"More?"

He lifted his bowl. I took it, refilled it, and put a little more in my own bowl.

He cut off a piece of bread and tore it in half, then began eating again like before, slowly, carefully.

It had been two weeks or a little more since I'd come away from my own house into his. When I'd wake up at night, on my bed in the main room, warmed by the stove, the walls seemed to lean in, dark and heavy. I missed the sound of Aunt Maura's steady breathing nearby, even the sound of Uncle Ted tossing on his bed in the attic.

Arden slept in the other room, which had a trapdoor leading down into the cellar storerooms. There was no door, but since I'd come he had hung a piece of heavy cloth across the opening.

He was quiet and gentle around me, even more than was his nature, I think. Maybe I just didn't expect that kind of gentleness after the stories. Maybe I didn't expect it of any man, except Ditsky, who was different. Arden didn't ask anything of me but that I read what I liked from among his books—I cooked and straightened up because I wanted something to do to feel useful.

One spring I had found a young robin, fallen from its nest into a pile of stones thrown out from the garden. I had made it a dark nest-place in a box, and fed it worms and mashed grasshoppers until it fledged and flew.

Sometimes at night I would wake up in the dark room and be startled by the difference of the walls around me and the way the bit of firelight gleamed around the iron lids of the stovetop. I felt then like that fallen bird, unexpectedly saved from among stones. I would realize where I was and go back to sleep.

"Done?"

I jumped.

"I'm sorry," he said.

"You didn't scare me. I was just—gathering wool."

"Wool-gathering?"

"I guess. Aunt Maura always said it the other way."

I took up my bowl and spoon, and his, and took them into the water room he had built on to the main cabin. A line ran down from a covered cistern on the hillside. The cistern was filled by a spring above it. Downhill pressure made the water run strongly through the line and, when a valve was opened, into a basin. It was more of a luxury than the books, even, not to have to draw up water every day.

I set the dishes in a pan of water. I would wash them up in the morning.

When I went back out, Arden had set the pot off the stove onto the side plate, and was stoking up the fire. A piece of pine or spruce popped and sparks flew out around him. The firelight flared orange and shone on his naked head and face.

"Would you like to read?" he asked.

"Yes."

It had become a regular thing. Each night, after dinner and before the weight of the day made us ready for sleep, I would read something aloud. Sometimes poetry, sometimes a story or a history. Arden then would talk with me about it and explain how the writer had put the words together to make the music of the writing.

He wrote himself, usually while I lay in my bed and seemed to be asleep. I would rest quiet and watch him at the table, bent over his journal, working under the light of a single candle.

"What is it you have there?" he asked. "Thoreau, isn't it?"

I nodded.

"Where are you now?"

"I'm reading *The Maine Woods*."

"It's been a long time since I read that. It would be fine."

I sat at the table, with the light, while he went out into the shadow of the room to sit in the big chair by the fire. I began where I had left off in my own reading, partway through the section called 'Ktaadn.'

"There it was, the State of Maine, which we had seen on the map, but not much like that,—immeasurable forest for the sun to shine on, that eastern stuff we hear of in Massachusetts. No clearing, no house. It did not look as if a solitary traveler had cut so much as a walking-stick there. Countless lakes,—Moosehead in the southwest, forty miles long by ten wide, like a gleaming silver platter at the end of the table; Chesuncook, eighteen long by three wide, without an island; Millinocket, on the south, with its hundred islands . . ."

The long, beautiful sentences rolled on, strange names, the distances, mountains where herbs grew that I had never gathered.

I paused and glanced over. He was leaning back the chair, his knotted hands loosely clasped on his stomach, his eyes closed.

"Are you tired?"

"No."

I began again.

"We were passing over 'Burnt Lands,' burnt by lightning, perchance, though they showed no recent marks of fire, hardly so much as a charred stump, but looked rather like a natural pasture for the moose and deer, exceedingly wild and desolate, with occasional strips of timber crossing them, and low poplars springing up, and patches of blueberries here and there. I found myself traversing them familiarly, like some pasture run to waste, or partially reclaimed by man; but when I reflected what man, what brother or sister or kinsman of our race made it and claimed it, I expected

the proprietor to rise up and dispute my passage.
It is difficult to conceive of a region uninhabited
by man. We habitually presume his presence and
influence everywhere."

"Do you think that is true now?" he asked,
coming in at the sentence pause.

"I think so. Even when I've been far back in
the woods, I've found things left by people. Bottles and shotgun shell-casings. And there are the
old roads and railroads, and paths."

"Those are things left by people, as you say.
But are people active on the land, a force as
Thoreau meant, cutting timber and clearing
farms, building towns?"

"Not here. I imagine so, other places."

He shook his head. "We have a new wilderness. Not the wilderness that William Bradford
found at Plymouth Plantation and called hid-
eous, and not the one that Thoreau knew. This
wilderness is one we made ourselves. A wilderness of broken things, abandoned things."

"Sometimes I have come across a rotten, old
barbed wire fence, running all by itself through
the woods, and then I feel like what Thoreau
said, about the people who made it."

"Sad?"

"That—and curious, too. About what the land
used to look like here, when those fences were
new."

"A lot of it was ugly," he said. "And a lot of it
was beautiful. This was my homeland, before I
moved to the city. These were my people who
lived here, but most of them didn't understand

how rare this country was, and getting rarer all
the time. They threw their garbage out by the
sides of the roads, they put up ugly buildings
with signs that blinked and flashed, they pulled
up coal and gas and oil from the ground and left
it scarred."

"The stream over the next ridge?"

"The one that runs red?"

"Did they all used to be like that?"

"That's mine drainage. Toward the end, at
least, that was less of a problem. They treated
the water when it came out of the mines. The
machinery is broken now, and the water comes
out of the mines polluted with the sulphurs
from the coal, the way it did years and years
ago."

"Oh." That red stream ran through bare stone
like a cut in the land. "Do you want me to read
any more?"

"If you want."

I read.

"*Perchance where* our *wild pines stand, and
leaves lie on their forest floor, in Concord, there
were once reapers, and husbandmen planted
grain; but here not even the surface has been
scarred by man, but it was a specimen of what
God saw fit to make this world. What is it to be
admitted to a museum, to see a myriad of particular things, compared to being shown some star's
surface, some hard matter in its home! I stand in
awe of my body, this matter to which I am bound
has become so strange to me. I fear not spirits,
ghosts, of which I am one,—that my body might,*

—but I fear bodies, I tremble to meet them. What is this Titan that has possession of me? Talk of mysteries! Think of our life in nature,—daily to be shown matter, to come in contact with it—rocks, trees, wind on our cheeks! the solid *earth! the* actual *world! the* common sense! Contact! Contact! Who *are we?* Where *are we?*"

I closed the book. I felt a trembling all through me. The words were wild, to speak so of the strangeness of breathing in and out every minute.

I turned toward Arden. He sat in the chair as before, his eyes closed. But now his hands clutched the arms of the chair, and his face was clenched against the pressure of some emotion which I couldn't name.

A chill came across me. I thought about what I had just read.

"I'm sorry. I shouldn't have read the last part."

He opened his eyes.

"'This matter to which I am bound has become so strange to me,'" he repeated, the lowness of his voice made even softer. "A hundred years true, a thousand—and I had forgotten it."

I sat at the table, unable to move, unable to take the book and place it back on the shelf. The trembling excitement of understanding Thoreau's vision had settled down dark and hard and cold in the pit of my stomach. The way that Thoreau was aware of his flesh and the way that I was, so different from how Arden must feel.

"I didn't mean to hurt you," I said. I wondered

if the sound reached him; he seemed a hundred miles away.

"You didn't, girl."

I was ashamed that he would have to deny the hurt I caused.

"Neena," he said. "I am used to my Change, within myself. Do you think I could have lived so long and not come to a settlement with this?"

I looked at him, then away.

"When you read that, I saw myself from your eyes, really for the first time."

"I don't notice, anymore."

"That isn't true. But I wonder at you, Neena Daucherty, that you at first saw through this—this alteration, this mask."

"It doesn't matter," I said, low, to myself, then realizing as I said it that it was true. "The handsomest things can turn out to be hateful, or dangerous. Like pokeberries. And other things can be good, things that are . . ."

"Ugly."

"Ugly." I swallowed the word. I remembered Uncle Ted, saying that the barterman was the ugliest thing I'd ever see. "I know that you can't trust the looks of something, or someone."

Then I realized that from somewhere there were tears in my eyes.

Chapter Seventeen

———◆———

THE STORM WAS cruel.

It came after two days of thaw, a spring-warm time when the melt ran down from the hills, even from the snow sheltered in the hollows of the northern slopes. The fields were silver with water flowing under the dead grass. The streams were choked with mud and with sticks and trash washed from the banks.

The rain started warm and soft before dawn. In the morning the wind changed, backing around from the southwest to the west. By mid-afternoon, it was howling down from the north-west, the rain driven into sleet, promising later snow. We had watched the weather change all through the day. When the wind shifted a quarter of the compass, we knew for sure there would be a bad storm.

Arden was dickering with a farmer who had come from the other side of Laurel Ridge. The farmer, who was tall but who had a slouched shoulder like an unhealed injury, stood with his back to the gusting wind and the sleet. His horse had its head down, nose to the icing grass. Its back steamed. Now and then the horse would lift its head, stamp, and try to move away into the shelter of the pines. Each time, the farmer jerked the reins and brought it around to a white-eyed, trembling stop.

The farmer wanted ammunition for the .22

caliber rifle that was slung in the saddle. He hadn't shown his barter yet.

Arden held his hand over his eyes, blocking the sleet. I could tell he was impatient with this man. Impatient with his slowness, and with the way he handled his horse, a fine-looking tall horse, chestnut with a blaze and its front legs white.

Arden nodded. The farmer turned into the wind and took down his saddlebags.

I came up behind Arden and stopped, balancing the load of wood in my arms.

".22 caliber long rifles," he said.

"How many?"

He nodded once.

The farmer started to unbuckle the saddlebags. I went inside, set the wood on the stack, then went into Arden's room and down through the trapdoor into the storerooms.

The storerooms took up more space underground than the cabin did above. They had been the basement of a house, long since gone, hand-cut sandstone blocks laid up and mortared. No one remembered the name of the family that had lived in the house that had fallen long before any wars.

Arden had rebuilt one collapsed wall and repaired the others, roofed part of the cellar over, then laid the logs for the cabin over the remaining cellar hole. Later, he built a tunnel from the cellar, a "bolt-hole" he called it, that came up inside the barn.

The cellar storerooms were dry and safe. This

was where he kept ammunition, in a big battered metal box, and also where the kerosene
was stored in a tank with a siphon pump, in a
little side room closed off with a plank door.

All around me, from the floor to the hewn logs
overhead, there were shelves loaded with coils
of wire, nails, chain, hooks, saw blades, sharpened and oiled tools for shaping wood and
metal. Other shelves held medicinals, many of
them ones that Aunt Maura and I had collected.
Furs hung from a line stretched along one wall,
beaver and muskrat and fox. There were metal
cans, glass jars, sieves, a thousand needful
things.

I went to the metal box. There were a few lacy
footprints of mice on its top—and two paw
prints where the big guard dog Lawyer had
leaped up to catch them. I opened the lid and
found the .22 ammunition. I took one box and
put it in the pocket of my jacket.

The sleet stung my face like fire when I went
back outside.

Arden held the contents of the farmer's saddlebags—two bundles of cured tobacco, a little
on the dark side, wrapped in worn plastic. I
handed the farmer his ammunition.

He held the box inside the flap of his coat and
counted the bullets, pulled them out one at a
time to look them over. They were reloads, of
course, but good ones. They wouldn't misfire,
nor blow up the barrel of the gun. Arden was
careful in his buying.

"Okay," the farmer said. "If they're any good,
I'll be back. The last I got was from a pack

trader out of the Line country, and they were no damn good."

"These are good."

"Say," the farmer said. "I'll be having that plastic back."

Arden unwrapped the first bundle and handed it to me, then the second. I held them inside my coat. He handed the plastic back to the farmer. It rattled in the wind.

"Hard to come by," the farmer said.

He put his foot in the stirrup and swung up. He pulled the horse's head around, nodded once in our direction, then urged the horse up to a stiff trot and was gone.

Arden looked after him. "I wish I had that horse," he said.

"Why?" He didn't have any stock animals, not so much as a chicken.

"So I could trade it to somebody who knew how to treat a good horse."

"This is bad weather to be traveling in."

"Bad weather for a hot animal to be left standing."

I rubbed the wet from my face with the dry lining inside my jacket. "I'm almost finished with bringing in wood."

"I'll check around the place."

He headed off toward the barn, where the large things like metal sheets and machine parts and sawed wood were stored. I went to the woodpile and gathered up an armload of mixed logs, cherry and oak and locust and poplar.

I was glad to be finished with the outside chores. I stacked the last armload near the stove and brushed the black crumbs of rotted bark from the arms of my jacket. A gust of wind drove against the solid logs of the cabin, rattling sleet and hard pellets of snow against the windows. It was almost dark. The wind soughed in the pines, a long, sad sound.

Another gust hit. The door opened and Arden came in, like he had been driven from the outside by the wind. The cold air pushed across the room as he held the door, and Lawyer came in after him.

"My friend and I could use a warm place by the fire, if the lady of the house allows," he said, his husky, Change-broken voice making it sound as if he were fatigued by a long run.

"I put some water on for tea."

"The lady is a queen, and this cabin a castle on a night like tonight."

I looked at him, but there was no mockery. His face and hands gleamed wetly as he stood, taking off his coat, then unbelting the holster and putting his pistol aside. He pulled out a chair and sat down to take off his boots, which were wet through.

The water was hot. I poured it from the iron kettle into the teapot, where I had already measured out the soothing catnip-based tea. (Tisane, I reminded myself. Aunt Maura said an herb tea is always a tisane.) I set the teapot aside to steep while I got cups and spoons, the jar of honey for sweetening, and a tray of muffins I had made earlier.

The thin-walled cups chimed when I set one down too hard. They were white as snow, edged with gold. I handled them carefully so as not to crack them, symbols that they were of all Arden's wealth. Wheat flour, beeswax candles, kerosene, ammunition—he had every luxury and necessity.

I filled the delicate cups and took one to Arden where he sat in the big stuffed chair in the stove-side corner. I stood close to the stove, warming myself inside with the tea and outside with my hands clasped around warm china and my back to the fire.

The wind drove against the house, and I wondered if the farmer and his horse had made it back over Laurel Ridge, or if they had holed up somewhere in an abandoned barn or house to wait out the storm. The way the darkness came on, I didn't see how they could have gotten very far.

Lawyer came padding in from the water room, where I had put down a bowl for him. He stood in front of me, panting with his tongue dripping water, his eyes half-closed.

I put my cup on the stove. "What does he want?"

"The rug."

I looked down at the braided rug I was standing on. The dog stared at it as though it might move. I moved away from the stove and sat down at the table.

Lawyer watched me sit down, then went to the rug, turned around twice, and lay down.

Lawyer was the biggest dog I had ever seen, so big that he was a threat just standing motionless, or even now curled up on the rug. He could stand and put his paws on Arden's shoulders. His fur was a thick grizzled brown, long, and longer yet where it grew into a lighter-colored ruff around his shoulders and neck. His head was big, with upright ears and a long, pointed, dark muzzle that was whitening with age.

He was also voiceless. The only sound he could make was a coughing whimper. He was silent in his rounds, trotting slowly from cabin to outbuilding, around the grove. He would lie in the shadows, watching everything that moved, watching me.

Now he lay with his head on his paws, eyes open and reflecting small the yellow flame from the candle on the table. His ears were cocked forward and twitched at every moan of the wind under the eaves.

"He hears everything," I said. One ear flicked back, then forward.

"I think sometimes he hears things before they happen," Arden said.

"Really?"

He motioned with his hand. "I shouldn't say that. But Lawyer is a wise animal, and he seems to be aware of trouble before it materializes. It goes beyond hearing and smell—though perhaps he smells the first traces of fear, or anger. That might be the physical explanation."

The dog's ears made the most delicate movements while Arden talked, as though the air that carried the words was being cupped inside them and tested.

"Have I ever told you how I came to find him?"

"No."

"It was in Washington." Arden leaned back in the chair. His face was out of the light. The words seemed to come from very far away in the darkness.

"It was after I realized that I would live. That took some time."

He paused again, gathering up the thread of his story.

"I had stayed at my college after the meta-chemicals were dropped—there didn't seem much point in running through the streets with the others. So I got beer from the student union and some food, and made myself comfortable in my office to wait. The Change came upon me."

Lawyer sighed, as though he understood.

"I thought that I could last out the pain, knowing that it would end soon. But it didn't end; I didn't die. The pain just went on and on. I couldn't walk. I dragged myself from office to office on that floor, looking for aspirin, looking through dead students' pockets for sinsemilla, anything to dull the pain. I found three tablets in the inside pocket of a jacket and took them. They were some kind of barbiturates. I swallowed all of them with a bottle of beer and I slept, but it seemed like I slept aware of the pain. And then I woke up again."

The cup was cool in my hands. I lifted it to my lips and sipped, a swallow of lukewarm tisane like grass in my mouth.

He motioned again, his knotted hand emerging from the shadow in his lap. "I survived. I may have been the only one in Georgetown. Later, near the Tidal Pool and on the White House lawn, I found sign that there were others —a few—who had lived after the metachemicals had altered their tissues.

"Once I knew that I was going to live, I left the college. I was too weak to walk far. I remember thinking that the stench of the bodies might be less elsewhere, but of course it wasn't. There were rotting bodies everywhere, rotting food in the markets, dead cats. Why did the metachemicals kill cats and not dogs, nor birds? The birds were everywhere. The city sounded like a forest, all the bird calls and no noise of traffic, no people to still them.

"I walked. It hurt just as much when I was still, so I walked. In no particular direction. I was near College Park when I met Lawyer."

The dog lifted his head and looked at Arden.

"My friend," he said to the dog. "Not right away, though."

"Were you afraid of him?"

"Afraid? Yes," and he laughed. "I came hobbling around the corner of a building and there he was, standing over some bloated thing with brown fur, another dog, maybe. It was about the right size. His ruff stood up all across his shoulders. He was about half-grown, and thin. His ribs and the ridge of his back showed through his matted fur, so that he looked like a wolf. I picked up a stick and backed against the wall. He flattened his ears and bared his teeth."

I shivered, knowing what wild dogs could do.

They were more dangerous than predators that were wild from the start because they weren't afraid of people.

"I shook the stick at him, and he bristled at me. I don't know how long we stood there. Then I realized how absolutely stupid it was. There I was, broken by the metachemicals, as good as alone in the city, walking among thousands of bodies, drifts of corpses—and I was shaking a stick at this dog, trying to protect myself. Trying to save my life! I threw the stick behind me. The dog watched it fall. And then I leaned back against the wall and laughed at myself, at both of us."

"What happened then?"

"He walked over to me, the fur still bristling, and just stood beside me."

"He didn't try to hurt you?"

"He stood there like he was waiting for a something, a command, maybe. I bent down and looked at his collar. There wasn't any name for him, just the owner's name and a telephone number. I said the owner's name a couple of times and he didn't respond. I slid the collar around his neck, unbuckled it and let it fall."

"Why did you name him Lawyer?"

"It used to be the practice in some areas to operate on dogs and cut their vocal cords, to mute them," he said, trailing off into some memory. He came slowly back, then laughed to himself. "When I realized that he could no longer bark, that was when I named him Lawyer."

"And so he stayed with you?"

"We slept under the same blanket, back to back for warmth, when we came over the mountains."

The wind slammed against the house. Lawyer raised his head and looked to Arden, then at me.

"He's suffered as much as we have, I suppose," I said.

Lawyer yawned, each white tooth gleaming as his lips pulled back.

He got up, stiff-legged, stretching forward and then back. He walked up to me and stood, the white tips of his long fur brushing against my leg.

I put my hand on his back. He was warm from the fire. There was a strong, carnivore odor from his fur, a smell of killing. I couldn't help but think of the wild packs I had heard and seen in the hills, dogs that had been pets and their young ones, old ones that remembered people and were not shy, the new generations that bred back toward the wolf, with yellow eyes and a strange, half-learned fierceness toward people and their livestock.

Lawyer pressed closer to my leg, then lifted his head and laid it on my knee. It was a warm, friendly, trusting weight.

"He's accepted you. Before he tolerated you. Now you are his."

"That's both ways," I answered. "I'm accepting him, too."

Chapter Eighteen

"**Where is he?**"

I jumped up, frightened half out of my mind. I looked around and saw the woman. She was wrapped in a long, brown coat. She stood at the edge of the grove, in the shadows, half-hidden by a tree trunk.

"Can you speak, girl? Can you understand? Is Barterman here?"

"Of course I can speak." I stood up and brushed the dirt off my knees. "You want to see Arden."

The woman frowned. "Barterman. He's the one I need to be seeing."

"I'll get him," I said, throwing down my trowel. "Don't be stepping on my diggings."

I looked around as I walked to the barn. Arden had taught me to be careful of ambushers and thieves—the woman might not be alone. The breeze blew freely through the pines, and it carried no sound nor scent of trouble.

I pushed open the door. It was dark after the afternoon light outside, dark and chill with the old winter air still closed inside.

"Arden?"

The light came across the interior in long streaks, diagonal from the gaps between the boards, falling across stored, salvaged things.

A tool fell. "Yes?"

"A woman."

He rose from behind the bulk of an old tractor

chassis, stripped now of its tires and wheels, steering mechanism, oil lines.

"I don't know if this hydraulic unit will work for what Hardesty wanted," he said, wiping grease from his hands and draping the rag across the green hood of the tractor. "I'm not sure, from the word he sent, what kind of machine it is he's trying to build."

"He should have come himself, maybe."

"It would have helped." He sounded tired. He came around the tractor, and we began to walk toward the door. "What does this woman want?"

I shrugged. "She didn't say."

"You don't know her?"

"She's new around here. She called me girl." I realized after I said it that I was still angry.

"Well, you are a girl."

"Not like she meant. She meant like—someone who wasn't right. Simple."

"Guilt by association."

"What does that mean?"

He didn't answer, but bent away from me to clear a low-hanging branch.

The woman stood where she had before, sheltered behind a tree.

"What do you bring, and what would you have?" he asked, straining his voice to make it carry to her.

The woman moved out from the shadow of the tree trunk. She had a face like an old tough banty hen, bright-eyed and suspicious. She held a deep basket in front of her, which from the pattern of oak splints and unpeeled willow withes I took to be Ann Skoda's work. Arden had several of those baskets in the storeroom, taken in barter. She reached into the basket and lifted out an egg.

"And milk," she said.

He walked closer. She stared at us, her eyes wild and white in her lined face. I expected her to duck back behind the tree, or run right away, but she didn't.

Arden held out his hand. She set the basket on the ground and stood back.

He bent down and picked up an egg from its travel nest of straw, a nice, brown egg with the bloom still on. There were maybe two dozen eggs in the basket. He set it back and lifted the milk jar, opened the lid, and smelled.

"Fresh," he said. "What do you want?"

"My man's needing a saw. A carpenter's saw."

He looked at her over the top of the jar.

"It's all we've got to barter," she said, not pleading, almost angry.

"Such things as saws aren't easy to come by."

She stood. The brown coat was gathered in at her waist with a strip of raw-looking leather; the coat wrapped halfway around her again, and the length of it sagged past her knees.

"I'll take the eggs and milk, and the basket."

"All?"

"Yes."

She nodded. Arden set the jar in the basket, lifted it up and went to the house.

As he turned away, the woman leaned to her left and spat three times on the ground, quickly.

When she turned back toward me, her face was twisted with hatred and fear.

I sat in the big chair beside the fire, sewing. I could not stop seeing the woman's face and feeling, like a blow against my body, the loathing.

He was the barterman, hardly human to her, a thing with a title instead of a person with a name.

I heard, like an echo, "Am I only Barterman to you all?"

It was how many weeks ago—how many days—that I had not had any other name to say but that? I remembered my own fear in a hot flush of shame.

My hands lay in my lap, the needle idle in the work, an incomplete stitch resting in a loop on the cloth.

There was so much fear in just living that I suppose I shouldn't still be surprised when that fear showed. Bombs and bullets might have killed, like in wars before, but the Change had come down on the people. It had driven the survivors of bombs and bullets from the cities and made it impossible for them to go back. Ever, I had heard said. No matter how many children were born now, they couldn't make the cold cities burn with lights again. When people saw Arden, they saw the end of their lives going on and on.

But the woman's hatred had not been just against Arden, but against me.

I heard the trapdoor open in Arden's room

and heard him come up, close it, and draw the rug over it. He lifted the door covering and came out. The lantern that he carried swung wild lights and shadows across the room.

"It will be beautiful," he said.

"Oh—do you think so?" I lifted the quilt-top and spread it across my lap. The colors seemed to flow into one another, red and blue and striped green, the points of the pieces scattering the light.

"What is that called—that pattern?"

"I don't know. Aunt Maura had one like it."

He went into the water room and hung the lantern from the hook above the basin. I heard the water gush through the opened valve into the basin, a hollow sound that filled up and became liquid.

I pulled the needle through, completing the stitch, knotted the thread and bit it off. The cloth smelled smoky, pressed close to my nose.

Arden had taken off his shirt. There was grease on his shoulder, a long, black gash of it that ran like a scar. He scrubbed at it with a wadded-up cloth. Water dripped onto the floor. There was the sharp smell of soap, mixed with the leaf-musk of damp skin.

The lantern light glistened on his skin like summer, and he was wet with sweat. The muscles moved in his back and shoulders and neck. Without any hair or beard, or hair on his chest, he looked oddly young, even with that bulk of his flesh. It really was difficult to tell how old he was, when usually the gray in a person's hair or the lines around his eyes tell you that.

I could see the strength in his muscles as he moved, his back broad enough to support the weight of a tree. His hands still looked swollen, but not greatly out of proportion, not like they looked when, at the end of shirtsleeves, they hung as though unconnected to his body.

Was it just that I was getting used to seeing him, that I didn't find him repulsive as others did? The Change rested on him like a birthmark or a withered arm rested on other people, a difference which, once it has been seen and recognized, was not frightening.

He put his shirt back on and came out to the fire. It had been a warm day, but the night air was chilly yet. He stood on the other side of the stove, buttoning his shirt, and when he looked up his eyes caught the light and shone, green and calm, like water that flows deep between canyon walls that darken but cannot hold the river.

Chapter Nineteen

———◆———

I DON'T KNOW what it was that woke me.

I came awake all at once. The house was quiet, and dark except for a thin slice of moonlight that reached from the crack of the shutters across the floor, almost to my bed.

Distantly, there was the thin treble singing of spring peeper frogs from the cattail swamp, and covering that sound the hoarse breathing of Arden in his own bed.

I rolled over. A crease in the bedding pressed across my stomach, and another one lower, across my hips. I rolled again, restless, the sheets and quilts pulling across my shoulders like a binding. I folded the pillow double and pressed my face against it.

In the other room, I heard Arden turn in his sleep and sigh the way a sleeping person does in the middle of the night.

I pushed back the covers and got up. The moonlight fell across me, and where it struck my skin was pale as the stars, pale as milk, pale as old snow against new grass. I shivered, and under my long shirt I felt the cool air and the nipples of my breasts against the cloth.

For a little while I stood in the middle of the room, in the white light, not sure why it was that I had woken up. Water, maybe. I walked out of the moonlight, toward the water room. Dirt gritted between the soles of my feet and the floor. I stopped, midway between the black

opening of the water room and the gray curtain
that hung across the door to Arden's room. I
could hear his breathing behind it.

I stood there and hugged my shirt close. I felt
chills and fever, the rapid coming-on of ague.

I lifted the curtain. The room was dark, light
seeping in around me and past the shutters on
the window. I stood there, afraid to move.

"I was called out of linen-wound sleep." The
fragment came into my mind. No, it was different, "Someone called out of linen-wound
sleep."

I remembered the maroon-cloth-covered book
where I had read that, a woman's writing. Most
poems were by men, about the way they longed
after women.

Then, as though the words were there in the
singing of the frogs, I heard it again.

> *Ecstasies built, brick and mortar,*
> *on the stealth of bare feet,*
> *someone called out of linen-wound sleep . . .*

Arden lay covered by the shadow-heaviness of
blankets. The bed was twice the size of mine
and pressed down by the weight of him. He
didn't know that I stood there, the night air cold
on me.

> *. . . to stand in a door*
> *and watch a face hollowed by the moon,*
> *eyes closed, saint's mouth open*
> *to taste of paradise—*
> *in dreams you outwait me, vigil-keeper, guard . . .*

* * *

I thought maybe long ago that woman, too, had stood in the doorway of a dark room. I wondered if the fire had wrapped itself around her breasts and her hips, as it did mine, the fire that I recognized from books and from poems, that I remembered from the whispered, urgent words of Uncle Ted and the first heat of his hand on me.

Arden gave no sign. I thought that he must in his sleep feel the difference, the space I took up there in the closed-in of the room.

I dropped the curtain and knelt beside the bed. His back was bare. I lifted my hand and put my fingers against his skin, and it was cool like the air, cool like remaining snow.

Movement, a sudden creaking and a flurry of blankets, and I felt his hand clench around my wrist and heard the metal-on-metal of a pistol being cocked.

"No," I whispered. It half-seemed that the word was still in my mind, not yet spoken.

"Neena?"

He sat up, his hand still on my wrist.

"It's me."

He let go. "What's wrong? I could have killed you, waking me like that."

I sat back on my heels.

"Are you sick? Hurt?"

"I don't know." A violent shudder went through me, and I leaned against the bed for steadiness.

"Here." He threw off the outermost of his

blankets and wrapped it around my shoulders. It was warm from his own body heat.

His face was close to mine as he pulled the blanket up close around my neck. I leaned forward just a little and touched my lips to his cheek.

He pulled back as though he had been burned. With the little light there was, I could see only the dark hollows of his eyes, colorless, hidden.

"Are you angry?"

He didn't answer.

I crept forward on my knees, and I put my hand on his where it rested outside the covers. He didn't pull his hand away.

"You should be back in your bed," he said, so low I could barely hear, even in the quiet, even near as I was.

"I woke up." There didn't seem to be anything else to say.

I lay down on the bed, on the narrow strip of space that was there, Arden not moving.

He put his hand on my arm, but it was a pressure, moving me away.

"Arden?"

"Yes."

"Are you . . . did the Change . . ."

"Am I a man, yet? Yes," he said. Maybe it was only the ordinary break of his speech that I heard. "And you are a girl, not a woman."

"I'm not a girl," I answered him. "I know."

"What?"

While I was looking for the words, the same line, again, like an answer. "'Someone called out of a linen-wound sleep...'"

"'My desire whetted to hazard edge on corundum days.'" His voice shook. "'Long-limbed I reach toward that sweet prize, knowing the height not beyond the grasp—the act of faith...'"

"Yes."

"Oh, Neena," he groaned, and he moved as he spoke, a kind of convulsion, an unthinking body-urge that I recognized. "You shouldn't be here. Go back. Go light the lantern and learn more poems, more words, just words. I can promise that I'll be your teacher in everything but this."

I could smell the leaf-mold smell of his skin, the musky sweat smell. The heat wound itself around my body until it was a fire on my skin.

I sat up and pulled off my shirt. The cold air stung my skin like a second fire.

Arden sighed. It was a sigh of acceptance. His hand lifted, rested an inch away from my body, then most delicately of all, his knotted finger brushed against the skin over my ribs.

I lay down. His skin was smooth as mine, but warm under the blankets, and the muscles moved under his skin like the rounded forms that iron-wood took under its smooth, pale bark.

His hand moved over my breast and I arched my back, pulled upward, fire pulled upward in a flame.

He was trembling, just like me. His hand stroked my breasts, softly, then down the length of my body.

He lifted himself above me, holding the weight of his body away from me with the strength of his arms. I spread my legs and his hips came down against mine, his man's hardness against me and his heat adding to mine. I felt a warm wetness between my legs. The muscles in my thighs trembled.

He lifted again. This time, he pressed against me, trying to enter, and I lifted myself toward him. A steady, pressing pain, the hardness of him within my softness. I felt I was being pushed down into the bed, down, pinned at my hips.

He pulled himself back, then pushed again, deeper inside me. I thought that I would tear, break open. For a moment I doubted him, wondered if the Change had scarred his manhood as it had his hands and face.

He pushed, groaned, and I cried out.

He rested there, above me, holding his weight from me. The thin light showed only the line of his shoulder and his arm.

He breathed in, shuddering, and rolled himself away. The cold air clenched around me, the sudden coldness of my bare skin and the wet warmth running between my legs.

"Neena? I didn't hurt you?"

"No," I whispered back.

He slid his arm under my shoulders, lifted me up and held me tight against him. I heard the slowing rhythm of his heart and the steady singing of the spring frogs, far away.

Chapter Twenty

———◆———

ONLY A VERY narrow road had run near the house when it was a house, a road wide enough for a single car.

In the first years of the war, the road must have been used by cars, trucks and walkers, people running from the cities, most of them not finding any place to go in the mountains. Then that road had grown up with weeds, followed by young trees which were now tall and straight in the ruts, like a new young forest guarded by the twisted old oaks that once had overlooked a road.

The house by which the road ran had been abandoned long before the road. When Arden came he went into the grove of pines and looked at the broken timbers fallen in the foundation. He built his cabin.

No one but people on foot and a few on horseback had traveled the overgrown road for years and years.

When the people came now, finding their way among the young trees, only a few were from the East and the great fallen cities. They were the scavengers who pried loose the useful scraps from the wreckage and brought them to Arden and to others who bartered the old for the new. Other people came from the West, from the little settlement that was Middletown on the bones of an abandoned city, or other small places. Overland they made paths, like the ridge path that I had walked. The roads all came to the grove.

The band came from the East. They were ten.

There was a man, and first I thought he had been Changed, like Arden, because his head was naked of hair or beard. His arms were hairy, though, and a shadowy dark stubble showed on his face and head. As he explained in a low voice like a secret between us, he shaved to be "like them that were gripped in the gray hand, they that be some in the old bone places, easy'st then to go among 'em."

He pulled a two-wheeled cart, standing between the poles like a horse. The cart was piled with clothing and cooking pots and the various things the band had picked up or traded for along the road.

There were two women with him, one whose hair was gray-streaked, one much younger. They each obeyed his orders, and I suppose were both his wives. They were equally dirty. The older woman reached inside her wrapped skirt and scratched herself as she looked at me.

There were children, numbering seven, from a black-haired baby at the younger woman's breast to a boy a little younger than myself. The children between wandered around the cabin, picking the daffodils that bloomed where they had been planted by the people who had lived in the house.

"Trade," the man called as he pulled the cart up by the door and set it back, its poles in the air. He called as if we were far away, though both Arden and I were not a pole's length from him.

"What have you?" Arden asked. And they began to haggle.

I went back to my work, setting lengths of horseradish root in a new bed I'd laid and bounded in with an arm's breadth of metal sheeting buried in the soil to check the spread of the fiery roots.

I laid the roots in horizontally, so that leaves would sprout up all along them.

"Yerr."

A child, I thought maybe three, pushed a broken daffodil toward me.

I reached out my hand, but the child pulled the flower away and smashed it in its fist. "Yerr."

"Yellow?"

The child nodded. "Yerr."

"I am Neena. Who are you?"

"Sen."

I couldn't tell if it was a girl-child or a boy-child. A brown bag-shirt hung from its thin shoulders to its scarred and dusty knees. There was a long, infected cut from left knee to ankle. One toe was black with dried blood.

"Sandra? Sean? Sienna?"

"Sen."

I decided that it was a girl. She took the flower that was in her hand and rubbed it against her cheek, leaving yellow streaks.

She stood there, the crushed flower still pressed against her face. Sen had muddy blue eyes and the kind of flat, unexpressive face that people sometimes have, but her hair was beautiful gold, even weeks-dirty, lousy, tangled with sticks and dead leaves.

"Dush'urt. Sick."

I couldn't understand the first part, but the second word was clear. Sick.

"Who's sick?"

"Dush."

She turned halfway around, as though she was bored, looking at the leafing trees and the flowers sprouting through the grass. She bent down and pressed her daffodil-sticky hand against the grass and smeared away the juice.

"Where's Dush?"

She held out her hand, and I took it and let her lead me. She went to the cart.

"Dush."

The man was gone to the outbuilding with Arden, and the women sat outside the grove in the sun, their eyes closed like they were just wanting a rest.

"Here?"

But the child was gone, already bent over in a daffodil patch, picking flowers. It was a girl-child.

I pushed back a lumpy sack of clothes or rags, or both. Under all the road-goods, there was a little space propped up with sticks and a length of cloth, a small closed tent, and in that space was a child. The child had shit itself, and not just once, not just recently. It lay in the yellow mess, not moving, breathing so shallowly that for a minute I didn't think it was breathing at all.

It might be influenza. Deeper inside, I knew it was cholera. I recognized it from the stink, and the way the child's eyes were sunk into the blue hollows of its face.

"Neena."

It was hot. I was lying on the bed in the hall with Herriot.

"Neena!"

Mom was in the bedroom, behind the closed door. There was a nurse with her. Herriot was with me.

There was a soft sound, the nurse talking, and Mom calling, calling like someone in a forest in the night. Sometimes it was my name she called, and sometimes it was West, who I knew was my father, and sometimes Kelly. Kelly was her mother, my grandmother, who was dead.

The nurse came out. She didn't look like the nurse in a picture book I remembered. She wore a gray sweater and a red shirt and pants that were too long and were turned up at the bottom and pinned. She closed the door behind her, looked at us squint-eyed, then went down the hall toward the kitchen.

"Neena," Mom called.

"I want to go in," I whispered, looking steady at Herriot so that she had to look back at me and answer. She threw her head back so that her blonde hair lifted away from her eyes.

"You better not."

"I want to. She's my Mom."

"You'll get sick! You'll die!"

I rolled off the bed and went to the door and pushed it open.

The room inside was half-dark, the blinds closed against the afternoon sun. There was a slice of sunlight across the wall from where a piece of the blind was missing. There was a bad smell in the room, and not all of it was from sweat and from the medicine.

"Mom?"

She mumbled something, but it wasn't my name.

I walked quietly across the floor. She lay there in the sheets; she didn't move.

Her face looked pale as the sheets. Her eyes were closed. I put out my hand to touch her on the cheek.

Her skin was hot, hot enough to burn me, and I pulled my hand away.

"Aieee!" She woke up. Her knees came up under the sheet and she rocked back and forth.

"Mom!"

"Aeeeeeeeee!"

Suddenly there was a hot rush of smell, an awful smell: blood and shit.

I thought I'd hurt her. I ran to the door and started to open it, but it came toward me, pushed by the nurse hurrying in from the hallway.

"Coming," she said, swinging the door out of her way and at the same time taking my arm and pushing me out of the room, out into the hallway where I stood, Herriot watching the whole thing from behind me on the bed.

Mom was curled up into a ball, the dirtied sheets wound all around her. The nurse took a

*cloth from a pan, wrung it out and began to
sponge her face and neck. She sponged her arms
and made them lie straight, pulled away the sheet.*

Mom looked up at the nurse. "Neena."

*The nurse didn't say anything. She lifted Mom's
nightgown away from her and kept sponging,
cleaning.*

*I heard her say again, "Neena." I ran into the
room, crying and shaking at the same time. I put
my arms around her. Her face was damp, like from
crying.*

*"We haven't got time for this," the nurse said as
she threw down her cloth and got up from the edge
of the bed. "There's people dying and I've not got
the time for babysitting."*

*She picked me up, right up, her hands under my
arms. I tried to take hold of Mom's hand, but it
slipped away from me, damp and hot and soft.*

"Mom! Mom!"

The child Dush kicked feebly at the light
which had come into its private little hole.

I stood there, trying to get free of the old
memories that I hadn't thought were still so
strong, memories that came back on me with a
turn of the light or a smell or a sound.

I wanted to run.

Cholera. The band was dragging death around
in the cart. I looked at the other children, and at
the women, thinking that I could see the flush of
fever and dehydration on their faces, the cramp
of pain in the way they held themselves.

I forced myself to think. First, tell Arden.

Then, get the medicinals that could help poor Dush, and the others.

I ran to the barn and got Arden aside, told him not to barter with the people because of the cholera and the sickness that might be carried in their clothing and the things they had to trade. The man watched us talk. He was anxious, fidgety, running his hand over the uneven stubble on his head and chin.

I left them and ran to the house, down the narrow ladder, and into the storerooms. There was a faint breath of air, wet with the earth-smell of the tunnel from which it had been pulled by the suction of the trapdoor opening. I pushed the herbs out of their neat rows, pulling out cranesbill root, dried berries of prickly ash, witch hazel bark. I piled them in a clean cloth square.

When I got back to the cart, the whole family was gathered around.

"Your child has cholera," I said, partly to the young woman and partly to the older one, not sure which was the mother. "I've got medicine to help."

"We got nothing to buy with," the older woman said. "He won't take trade." She glared at Arden.

The man stood between the poles, ready to pick them up and leave. The breeze blew back to me the smell of the sick child.

"I'll give this to you." I opened the cloth. "This root is geranium maculatum—you might have heard it called cranesbill or alumroot. The berries are prickly ash. They're the best medicines against cholera. Boil water, then set these in the pot and let them steep, to draw out the good part into tea. Boil the witch hazel bark to make a wash to bring down the fever."

The younger woman pulled her ragged sweater up around her shoulders. Pulled tight, it made her look even skinnier. She went to the cart and looked at the child, a long, studying look.

"My Dustin," she said. "I got drugs."

I stood there, holding the cloth. Maybe she already had the specifics, from somebody else.

"There's a good place to camp, with water, a ways down the old road. A good, sheltered place, where you can take care of the child."

"We go as we want," she said. "I take care of Dustin. See."

She put her hand down into the corner of the cart, among all the jumbled-up things, and somehow came up with a little box that she held up in the air.

I reached for it, and she pulled it back and held it close to her chest.

"Mine," she said harshly.

She pushed back the lid of the box and began to pull things out. It was packed tight. She worried at a piece of stiff plastic until it came loose from the rest.

"See," she said, and held it up.

There were little round pockets inside the plastic, and each pocket was filled with a pink powder. Some of the pockets were empty. Some of the pockets were only half full.

"What is it?" I asked.

"Medicine," she crowed. "Not roots. Old medicine. New then."

"Pepto-Bismol tablets," said Arden. "You used to buy them in stores, for stomach aches."

"Are they any good?" I asked.

"Not against cholera. Then or now."

"Good medicine," the young woman said, pushing the plastic back into the box as if I was going to take it away from her.

She was sure that the old medicine was best. I didn't know what to tell her, how to help. I thought about the band traveling through the area, spreading the disease, dying from it, and others dying.

"Please," I said. "Take this, too. It will help, with your medicine."

The man picked up the poles. "Be going," he said.

"Please." I wrapped up the cloth and set it on the cart.

The old woman went out in advance, the younger woman walking behind the cart and the children wandering as they wanted. They walked out of the grove, heading west. The white cloth showed on top of the load, untouched.

"Do you think they'll use it?"

Arden watched them move away. "No."

"Was I stupid to give them the herbs?"

"No," he said. "A person can't do any more than that, any more than offer."

Chapter Twenty-one

———◆———

Arden's Diary
March 25

SPRING HAS COME, according to the passage of
the sun past equinox, but the season lags behind.

I look forward to the coming of spring, the
first season I have greeted with my heart for
time past counting. I see the swelling of the
buds on the trees, the leaves growing and
bursting the brown scales, and my own soul
swells with these, is impatient with the same
rising sap. For too long I was like the pines
that shelter this house, enduring from season
to season, year to year, my growth marked
only in the hardening of a new enclosing ring
of protection.

It is Neena who has done this. As I sit writing, she moves about the room, giving off
warmth like a spark from the flame of her
hair.

For myself when I am old and my memories
lose their brilliance, or for others who may read
this:

Neena Daucherty is moderately tall, 5'-8" perhaps, small-breasted and slender-hipped. She
moves gracefully, with the grace that comes of
long walks, daily labors. Her hair is fiery red,
and worn free it frames her oval face and ripples
down her shoulders in repeated waves. Her

skin is fair, milk white on her stomach and breasts, lightly freckled on her hands, arms, and face, where the sun has reached. Her eyes are the color of the wild iris that grows in great circling beds near the pond, a clear blue, and while by no means innocent, her eyes do not reflect the deepness of the shadows that I have seen in my own eyes, in so many others'.

My thoughts turn naturally to the superlatives that others have written, but I will not cheapen her own unique beauty by framing it within the descriptions of another.

It has been my joy to be her teacher, first, and to guide her mind in learning. That joy, which had faded in classroom routine and which seemed to have been lost permanently with the wars, has been reborn. Neena hungers for knowledge. Often she surprises me with the depth of her understanding. She remakes concepts into the likenesses of her own world, working similes from the woods and fields that are fresh and apt.

This would be enough—more than I could have ever desired—to hear and see Neena at work, to talk with her over books at the end of the day. Enough to have thawed my personal, long winter.

Never did I think to be more than her guardian and teacher. Not when I took her from Ted on that January hillside, did I hope, even think, of more. That she herself could come to love me, as I am, is a daily surprise, and as much that I daily lose myself in returning her love.

My mind casts over the love stories of the past 2,000 years, and all seem wanting. We are born new, phoenixes. Without the ashes, could there have risen this fire?

Chapter Twenty-two

———•———

TRILLIUMS FOAMED DOWN the hillsides like water.

Where the swales cut, on the steep banks sloping down to little streams that disappeared in summer, the trilliums rooted and bloomed, and the dark wet soil was white with them. Every now and again there was a purple blossom, or smaller ones which tended to a greenish yellow.

I wondered how these flowers had come to be called wake-robin, since the robins were around in great flocks before the trilliums showed.

The other names went through my memory— birthroot, bethroot, ground lily.

And the values, for coughs and for fever, and for use when there was blood in the urine.

It wasn't the trilliums I was after, not this early, though later I'd remember this patch for harvesting the root. I was wanting early greens

—shepherd's purse, young dandelion leaves, peppergrass, dock, sorrel—and here in the woodlands, ramps. After a long winter, spring brought a hunger for fresh things, the crunch of green leaves.

The wind was changeable, shifting around from west to south and back, swirling. It lifted last year's leaves up from the ground in spirals that twisted halfway around and collapsed. The onion odor of ramps was in the wind, but it was hard to tell direction. I crossed the swale and went down into the bottom, where the soil was moist and rich and likely for the wild leeks.

Below and beneath a tangle of raspberry canes and greenbrier, I found them. The wide green blades were bright against the gray-brown of the leaf litter, as strong a color as their smell and taste.

I took the pointed trowel out of the collecting basket and set to work. The soil was loose and the bulbs came out easily. I shook the dirt from them and laid them along one side of the basket, folding back the cloth to keep the other side neat for the greens that I'd pick on the way home.

A stick snapped, somewhere up above.

I stopped digging and stayed still. The brier-brush was thick above me.

It was quiet. Not the normal quiet of a woods, which means the sound of birds and mice and insects, but the quiet when someone has intruded.

Slowly, I pushed the shiny blade of the trowel into the ground. I reached into the basket and put my hand on the pistol that was under the cloth. It was loaded with shells made up with snake-shot, hardly something to kill a person, but the pellets could hurt. Or blind.

Whoever it was started down the slope. Not fast, so he couldn't have seen me yet. There were gouged places on the hillside where my heels had dug in, track enough to follow.

I waited, still as still, the gun cocked and ready but hidden.

The noise stopped, right outside the briers. Looking through the stems, I could see boots. Dark brown leather, laced, familiar, familiar as the worn boots on my own feet.

"Neena?" He began to circle the briers. It wouldn't do to hide any longer.

I stood up. I held the basket on my arm. I turned around to face him.

"Hello, Uncle Ted."

"Neena."

His hair was longer. He wore it pulled back and tied, like Ditsky. It showed his eyes more that way, and I tried to read them but the emotions were mixed.

"I saw you walking," he said.

He must have been up on the opposite ridge. What was he doing there? Watching, I guessed. Just watching.

"Your hair looks like a torch, even from away."

"The wind."

He smiled. "Aren't you going to come out of that brier patch?"

"I'm digging ramps."

His smile faded, slowly. He looked thinner, as though the winter had bitten the flesh from him.

"You act like I'm a stranger."

"I don't mean to."

"Then come out of there and let me see you." He stepped forward and reached out his hands. "I'm still your Uncle Ted."

Now I could read his eyes. That same hunger, shining there, mixed with something more like to fear than caution.

"I think it'd be best if we left things as they are," I said.

"Neena?"

"No, Uncle Ted."

"Uncle Ted, Uncle Ted," he mocked. "That's Maura's doing. She drove you away. I tell her that, too, that she drove you away for no reason, no reason that holds true now."

His hands, still reaching, shook. He looked as if he had been chased there, to me, his face pale and sweating, the scar showing.

"You did a lot for me. You brought poetry to me, something I didn't know about, that kind of beauty in the words." I tried to find words to calm him. All the time, my hand sweated against the cloth that covered the pistol and I wondered if I would be able to use it, if I had to. "You're my only family except for Aunt Maura, and I love you for that."

"Do you love that—man—like you do me?"

"Arden."

"Him."

"No, I . . ."

Before I could continue there was a passing of triumph across his face.

"It's not the same thing. I love Arden as he is, not for what I thought he'd be, or for what I might have tried to make of him. I love you in a different way, my Uncle Ted. When you first came here, I thought that I loved you more than anyone."

"You still love me," he said, low, the words harsh against the tightness of his throat. He swallowed hard. "He stole you, to hurt me. I don't know how, but he lured you away and you went."

"It was time I went."

"Do you let him touch you? Tell me that he doesn't touch you."

I stared back at him, hoping that I looked steadier than I felt.

"Come with me. You can't tell me no." He stepped forward. His trembling hand was within the length of my own reach back, if I'd wanted.

"I won't come with you, Uncle Ted."

"Neena." He leaned closer; his hand was inches from mine. I could smell the familiar tobacco acids on his breath.

"You have to understand. I went to him. I went to Arden, to his bed at night. I chose to. If there was marrying, now, I'd be his wife."

The last color drained from his face and he swayed, looking to be close to fainting.

I pushed through the briers to the right, not caring if they tore my clothes and through to my skin. I brushed past him and walked quickly up the slope and onto the faint deer trail that led home.

Lawyer greeted me when I came into the grove by lifting his great, gray muzzle in my direction. He must have nosed my sweat, or maybe there was some smell of Uncle Ted carried onto me by the wind when we had stood there close, because he got up and padded into the house behind me.

I set the basket on the table.

Arden came out from the bedroom. He held a delicate mechanism in one hand, a small screwdriver in the other.

"You didn't have to hurry," he said.

"I did."

I told him that I had met my uncle, that he had watched and followed me. I told him what he had said. It made me angry to be retelling the things Uncle Ted told me.

"It's somewhat true."

I pulled out a chair and sat down, to catch my wind and my calm.

He sat down across the table, still holding the mechanism cradled in the wide hollow of his hand. It looked like the inside of a pump.

"I can admit it now, though I wouldn't have then, even to myself, that I took you away partly because I wanted to protect you, because of what I knew about him, and partly because I wanted very, very badly to hurt him. And I did."

"Did it help?"

"No." He stared down at the mechanism.

My anger pushed me to my feet, and I paced between the book-wall and the door. I felt like a little girl, not knowing what her elders thought.

"Was I something to be bartered, haggled over?"

"Neena."

"Didn't I count in this thing?" I was hot, sweaty-palmed. "Was I just something to be won, between you two men?"

"Neena."

I glanced at him and saw that he still sat, stock still, and I wished that he would move, stand, crush the little metal thing in his fist.

"I cannot say it was any different than it was. Out there, in the snow that night, facing Ted. After the first satisfaction of having taken something from him—at the time it seemed an immense satisfaction—there was nothing different. But you."

He raised his head, and in his gray-green eyes there was a glowing spark of a hunger like the spark I had seen in Uncle Ted's, but clean and open.

"You are my love, all of my life, Neena Daucherty. You have gathered me in like those plants in your basket."

I felt myself blushing, to be the focus of, to be permitted to see, that naked need.

"You still didn't know?" I shook my head in answer.

"Our motivations are always so mixed," he said. "Humans aren't a clean animal, any way that you choose."

I stood up and began to empty out the basket.

I laid the ramps on the table, and the few greens that I had forced myself to gather when I was in sight of home, now limp and dark.

I lifted out the cloth and laid it on the floor, until I could shake it out. I took the pistol out and laid it on the table.

The light gleamed on the barrel. It was clean, and it had one purpose. The grip was worn from the pressure of Arden's hand, and somebody's before him. Hands that had held the pistol, with its one purpose, and each person that had held the gun had so many different purposes pressing inside.

"Did he know you had the gun?" Arden asked.

"I don't think so, no." I touched the barrel, cold steel. And I wondered.

Chapter Twenty-three

IT HAD RAINED during the night.

The grass was wet, and sparkling with drops that were held on the tips of the blades. The sun shimmered in the grass and glowed through the wet, young leaves of the trees. In the garden the sun glowed, too, captured green in potato leaves and hollow onion tops and the quills of sprouting corn.

The sky was clear except in the northeast, where the last purple of the rain clouds showed like a second, newly heaped-up line of a ridge.

My path crossed Arden's as I walked to the barn. His tracks, dark green in the silvered wetness, went from house to barn and then back through the grove and out, across the line of the old road and on to the young woods. There was a second line beside his tracks, where Lawyer had walked beside him and then turned back at the edge of the trees.

I listened; there was no sound but the bluebirds singing, and the summer call of the chickadees in the pines. Then I heard a crack of wood broken. Arden was cutting limber young saplings for me to weave into a trellis for the runner beans.

I had a thousand things to attend to, the first of which was to set out the rhubarb roots that we had taken in barter from Frank Glover. He had come at the first light, wanting nails.

The air was sweet and soft. It felt good on my bare arms, like the sun.

I went into the barn and found a planting spade and a hoe. There was weeding to do, the violets and chickweed sprouting like mad in the garden rows. Once I had been gentle about violets, not wanting to uproot the heart-leaved plants and the purple blossoms. Then I learned how stubborn the plants are once they're well started in cleared ground. I'd save and dry the leaves and flowers, but even though they had their uses, the violets had to go.

Lawyer was waiting at the door when I came out. He stood with his nose into the wind.

"Company?"

He answered by looking up at me and then away.

We waited together. Finally, my ears caught a banging, rattling sound, yet far away, almost like a birdcall.

The scavenger arrived in his own good time. He carried a pack and pulled a larger burden strapped onto a pair of long poles that dragged the ground, a travois. He was shaven badly and recently, except for a drooping mustache. His eyes, which were the same flat brown as his hair, were reddened from staring into the sun and wind.

He had a long, heavy-bladed knife hanging from a strap at his waist, and the sun sometimes glinted on the sharpened edges where they showed above the sheath.

But the sun had other places to shine. The man wore everywhere bits and pieces of the insides of old dead machines, some strung on a thread like a necklace, others with their wires pushed through pierced places in his earlobes and even his nose. The wire shone, gold and silver, and the little rounds and triangles and squares had their own colors of black, striped brown, yellow and red.

"Hi'an firsting eh you," he said.

He shifted something in his mouth; it was brown but didn't look like tobacco.

"Barter'an—yer know where?"

"H-h-ere," I stammered, not able to stop looking at the decorations that wiggled and glittered all over him, even wrapped and twisted into his greasy brown hair where it curled by his ears.

"Here?"

"This is our—his—place. I'm Neena."

"Neena." He shifted from one foot to the other, and the pieces brushed against each other, thin ghosts clacking. "Barter'an be wanting."

"I can trade with you," I said.

"Wellan good." He dropped the poles of the travois. "Come an from Big Bay."

"Baltimore?"

"An too." He shifted the wad in his mouth and spat on the ground.

"What do you have?"

"Anty for me. Trading is'ta scribblers."

I know I must have looked puzzled. His talk was strange, but so was other people's talk, people that came from the coast. It seemed like the metachemicals had created new words and twisted the old ones.

He shook his head. The danglers twinkled. He bent over the travois and carefully unwrapped just the center of the bundle. He rattled around there for a moment and then pulled out a handful of bright yellow pencils.

"Scribblers," I said.

"Ya."

He pulled one from the bundle and handed it to me. It had never been sharpened. The lead was a perfect round dot in the center, the wood that surrounded it cut into a perfect, six-sided tube. The eraser was the same fuzzy type of red that I remembered. I looked at the side. "No. 2," stamped in gold. Farther down the side, "Silver Springs Landscaping," also stamped into the wood.

I could think of people who wanted pencils. Starting with Arden, and me.

"What do you need?"

"Nothing."

"Nothing?"

"Need nothing. Want'in things."

He didn't volunteer any more. Finally, considering the likely value of the pencils, I began to name things—cutting blades, wire, rope. He shifted from one foot to the other, his hipbone jutting out.

"Whiskey?" he asked at last.

"No." All of Uncle Ted's was long since traded.

"Said barter'an as whiskey."

"It's gone, what we had. What about tobacco? Or medicines?"

"Ant'a those." He laughed, and broken teeth showed all along his upper gum. "Hain'tha need. An fever stay witha manypeople, an t'squats. Haint afcar es Change."

"No? Why not?"

He shook his head and the bits danced. "Know the Gray Paths, the White Paths. Follow an White Paths, inta cities. No not the bones af'ta Gray Paths. Be sav'in, not ta touch, no not stay. An bonelets save." He stroked the shiny glass and metal ornaments strung around his neck.

I understood part of it, knew that the scavengers had their own routes into the cities, and that many—some, anyway—went in and out without falling into the Change.

"You came from Baltimore, you said. Did you come through Hagerstown?"

He stared at me like the city, and the name of the city, no longer existed.

"Hager Camp," he said slowly.

"You were there?"

"An not es place for head n'feet. Was end-winter in'ta lockyup a Hager Camp." He coughed, not a real cough, but a symbol or a code. "Hard place, an that. Forties an fifties af soldiers, greencoats, an t'poor walker they take down. Is'ta winter in lockyup, hard bread, hard bunk, hard labring."

"Did you hear of any Dauchertys? Leveauxs? Andersons?"

He laughed, showing those broken teeth, and he put his hands up and shook an imaginary fence, tilting his head to look past imaginary bars.

In my mind I heard marching feet, orders. Hagerstown a military camp. I wondered where Herriot was now. I wondered about Ofalia.

"Did you see any women like—one that looked like me?"

He shook the fence again.

"Have seen t' hard roads, towns that way-round I go, but Hager Camp . . ."

Slowly, he let his hands down.

"Well." I stared at the drifts of yellow mustard and buttercup until the lump went away from my throat. My own foolishness, to be asking.

"Well. What will you have?"

He studied the toes of his boots. They were old, broken soldier boots, several times patched on the toes. They had soles of rawhide wrapped up moccasin-style. The stitching gaped along the seams and was pulled roughly together.

"Shoes?"

"Have'n boots?"

I thought about the pencils. I thought about the rows of shoes and boots on the second shelf on the back wall of the cellar storage. There was a matched-up set, not too worn, about his size.

"I think so. Give me one, to check."

His mouth pulled down, distrustful, tracing the same curve as his mustache.

"What would I be wanting with one old boot?"

He bent down, unlaced his left boot, and handed it to me. He had strips of gray cloth wound around his feet. They were stained where the weather had come in at the broken seams.

I left Lawyer to watch him.

As I had thought, the boots (they weren't really a pair, but close) were nearly the same size, maybe a half a size larger.

I handed him one to try, and he pulled it on and drew the laces tight. He lifted his foot, twisted it this way and that, the way a person might turn this way and that while looking in a mirror.

"Fair?" I asked.

He grinned and kicked his new-booted foot high into the air. There were black oblong things fastened to the cloth of his pant leg by many little wire pins on their undersides.

He handed me the rest of the pencils, and I gave him the other boot. He laboriously untied the broken laces on his old boot, took it off, and set it on the grass, then put on the new boot. The old boots leaned against each other, just tired.

"An fine," he said. "Fine."

"I'm glad."

He stood there for a bit. I could see him wiggling his toes in the new boots.

He bent his head down and seemed to be looking for something on his shirt—a red cylinder attached to a hole in his shirt front by two metal spikes on its bottom which were bent around. He unfastened it and handed it to me.

"For barter-Neena." He smiled a broken smile.

He picked up the poles of the travois and walked away, out of the grove and down the road. Finally, all I could see was the top of his head, bobbing along against a background of yellow mustard in the field.

I turned the red thing over in my hand. It was smooth to the touch; on the side an angular symbol was faintly marked in white.

I put it in the buttonhole of my collar and bent the prongs around to hold it.

"Back to work," I said to Lawyer. He whined softly and looked up the road, then down.

Chapter Twenty-four

———◆———

THE BEST TIME to gather medicinals was in warm, dry weather. That was a given for all types. But flowering parts were best taken when they opened in the morning, and after the dew was gone off them. Fruits like rose hips should be picked when fully ripe. Roots from annual plants were to be dug before flowering, perennials in the fall or winter.

So it fell that year around, from early spring to the hard-ground dryness of December before snow, there was a time to be picking and digging and drying and storing.

High summer, now, and the fields and woodlands were thick and green with growth, hundreds of plants growing singly or in bunches, or carpeting whole stretches of ground, and most of them had a use, or several. The old month-names of June and July and August didn't seem adequate, when time was paced by the flowering of boneset, lobelia, and yarrow.

I shifted the basket on my left arm, lifting the handle from where it had made a dent in my skin. I felt a little leg-tired and breathless from the walk, and thought that maybe I had been spending too much time in the house, in the grove.

Clouds drifted overhead. The sky was clear blue, not a trace of haziness. A faint breeze rippled in the treetops, fluttering the leaves from green to underside-silver. A fine day, and my baskets were half-heavy already with wilting flowers and with raspberries picked from where vines crept over the ruins of an old side-split barn. As soon as I had gathered the yarrow-bloom that was the real reason for the outing, I would have to turn back. There were house chores waiting, a garden to be weeded, beans to pick, tomatoes to prune and tie up, but none of the chores seemed too heavy on such a day.

Yarrow, which had many uses beyond wound-binding, grew thickly in an abandoned meadow not far from the barn where I'd picked raspberries. The people had tried to make a go of it, but the farm was so isolated, visitors so infrequent. When a pack peddler came there a couple of years ago, he'd found a burned house and the people, who I think were named Hebner or Hadner, were gone. The strange thing was that there hadn't been any raiders around. The outbuildings still held tools and implements, and the cattle and goats were wandering freely.

The meadow where the cattle used to graze would be forest, soon enough. Sassafras and rock maple and locust were seeding out from the forest edges. First seedlings, then saplings, then a forest. Eventually a fire, set by lightning, and then meadow again.

I crested a rise and looked out over the meadow. It was white with yarrow, mingled with purple-red clover blossoms, yellow mustard and dandelions, orange butterfly weed, and the bright disks of daisies and black-eyed Susans. The breeze bent the heads of the grasses over, a wave passing from west to east.

A killdeer flew up and began to circle, mewing, a sad sound even on a summer day, saddest in the fall. I followed its circling, then looked to see where it had been startled from, and why.

Someone else was in the yarrow field. All that was visible was the curve of a bent, brown back. I didn't have to look closely to know that it was Aunt Maura's.

She came up from her work, pressing her hands into the small of her back, and she watched the killdeer fly, the sun on the black bands of its breast and on the rapid beating of its pointed wings. Her eyes also followed its circling. Her glance tired, fell like a leaf, and came to rest on me.

She stood up, still half-bent from her work. Her back must be giving her more trouble, I thought.

"Daneen," she called. The killdeer circled, crying.

I stood among the trees, not sure what to do. She stood hip-deep in the hay, waiting, patient.

I hitched the basket farther up my arm and went down into the meadow grasses. Bindweed caught at my feet, but it was not the only thing holding me back, making me walk slowly. I tumbled from one feeling to another: sadness and happiness and disappointment and fear. Not fear—unsureness. It came back, strong, as though it had never left me, that paralyzing sense of not knowing what to do. All the changes inside me suddenly were gone, wiped out, forgotten.

I went to her. I saw that she, too, was stiff with unsureness, and I was surprised. It seemed like it had been years, many years, since the cold of January. I shivered to remember.

"Hello, Aunt Maura," I said. The words were strangled as they came out.

"You look well."

"You do too."

The aroma of the grasses and plants came up from where our feet had stamped them down. A green, sharp smell. I could pick out the individual songs of the grasshoppers nearby.

"We never had time to talk," she said abruptly.

"About what?"

"About ..." She gestured with her free hand, which was stained green from plucking the blossom-heads from yarrow. "Things sort of ran away from me. I haven't done much to catch up, either, I guess."

She sat down, and then I did. The hay stalks rose all around us.

She hadn't changed much, though her hair seemed to be a bit whiter. She had it pulled back tightly in a knot at the nape of her neck. The sun was full on her face, and it showed all the lines and wrinkles, the flaky places where her skin was dry on her forehead and nose. It highlighted the line of her jaw, and I realized, I suppose for the first time, that her face was shaped like my mother's. And my own.

Fascinated, I began to see the way her nose looked like Uncle Ted's, but not like mine, nor in a different way like my mother's. Earlobes, they were alike. Aunt Maura's eyes, though they were brown, had a certain shape and a fold at the corner that made them look sleepy, and I recognized that.

Family. It wasn't something to be picked up or put down, just like that. It stayed with you. It followed you, showed in the way you walked and the way your children walked. I knew that I had missed that kind of closeness, that the bond between Arden and me was strong and good, but that this bond was first and was under it all like stone under soil.

"Is he good to you?"

The question startled me. "Oh, yes. We read a lot together. I help with the bartering, sometimes, and I have a garden."

Her brown eyes seemed to be asking something more, and for no good reason I looked away.

Aunt Maura sighed and began to tie knots in a stem of grass. She pulled too tightly, and the stem split lengthwise and broke apart.

"I'm sorry," she said.

"For what?"

"That I couldn't do something about my brother before it all came to this. This splitting."

"It would have happened, someday," I answered, the words coming from somewhere. True words, I realized at the same time I said them.

"It was hard, the way it happened." Aunt Maura looked at me with a searching look. What was she hoping to find in my face? What had she already found?

"I love Ted," she said. Just plain and quiet. "I love him, and I can't change that."

She pulled another hay stem from its sheath and began to tie knots. Her fingers trembled.

"He had his faults when he was a boy. He was hard-headed, always doing the wrong thing and then too stubborn to admit it. I don't know how many scrapes I got him out of, and there were more that I didn't know about until it was too late.

"He never took any punishment for the mistakes he made. He always got away, from mother, from the school authorities. And he was bright, from the word go. He could make up stories that would hang together just long enough—they always were good for just long enough."

There were five knots in the stem in her hands. She stared down at the knots, each oozing green plant juice.

"I promised I'd do my best by you when Ditsky brought you to me with the message from Terra. I'm not good with children, I never was, but I tried. I don't think there were any problems, until Ted came. I soon learned what he'd been at, what he'd been doing on the coast, and it just sickened me. He might as well have come in the door with blood on his hands—it didn't matter, I couldn't turn him away. And then, when he began to pay attention to you, first I wouldn't admit it, and then when it was in the open, I couldn't do anything about it. I was just helpless."

The single clouds were larger now, closer together. I focused on one drifting near the horizon. I couldn't look at Aunt Maura. I couldn't believe that she was saying that she was helpless—not Aunt Maura.

"We had an argument, a couple of weeks after you left. Really a bad one. I can't remember what started it, but then I asked him why he ran away, like always, why he hadn't stayed and used his knowledge to make the metachemicals harmless." She coughed.

"He got quiet, cold as ice, and then he told me in very great detail how the metachemicals work, and why any tampering with them would just make it worse. That even now, the weather was changing the chemicals, the original ones and the ones made in the splinter labs. Wind picks up the dust particles and moves them, combining ones of different types, altering them. Nobody knew what would happen in the sun and the rain and the cold. Nobody *knew*. There might be plagues riding around in the clouds, waiting to fall with the rain."

The fluffy, white cloud wasn't so harmless. I saw a cloud shadow roll across a neighboring meadow. I hugged my arms around myself and felt threatened by the passing shadows.

"You know, the metachemicals became the weapon of choice, the ones we stockpiled when nuclear arms were banned," she continued, talking to herself more than to me. "Metachemicals don't destroy cities, or croplands. They kill people and then, after a while, they're gone. A long while, and it looks like a lot longer than they predicted, but not as long as radiation. They say. God, did we ever think we'd be using them on ourselves?"

That last cry, like the cry of the killdeer, and then Aunt Maura hung her head and began to sob.

I put my hand out and touched her on the shoulder. Such a long way, it seemed.

"Aunt Maura..." I leaned closer and put my arm across her heaving shoulders. "It's all right. You couldn't help it."

She shook her head.

"I knew. I heard some things. I knew part of it. You can't help it that you love him. I loved him, too, except it got all twisted up with the other. I knew, but I didn't want to know. Like when he came back that day, and there was blood on him, and I couldn't believe. Not for the longest time could I believe."

Her sobs lessened and she sat up. Her eyes were dry. She hadn't let go of all the pain, just a little of it.

We sat among the grasses, two people, family, but I knew that we were still divided. Uncle Ted stood between us, just as surely as if he had been there. There was so much that I wanted to say to her, to ask, but his shadow hung between us like the threat of a storm.

Finally, Aunt Maura pushed herself up. She took her basket and put it on her arm.

"Aunt Maura!" I couldn't let her leave, not yet. "I—I have something to tell you."

She waited. Her eyes were patient. Like windows, they had been closed up again. They had the familiar outward look of patience over the pain that came through for a little while.

"I think I'm pregnant," I said in a rush. My heart was pounding.

"Arden?" she asked, her voice disturbingly full of wonder and disbelief and shock.

"Aren't you—well, his child..." she said, limply.

"He knows about the metachemicals. He has a book on them," I explained. It was like reassuring myself, as I had at first with the strange scientific words in that book. "They work in the endocrine system, and on the parts of the body that grow, like the ends of the bones. It's not the same on everybody. But anyway, they don't hurt the inner parts, the cells in the sex parts."

She nodded, as though she understood all of it, somehow more than I did.

"Does Arden know?"

"I haven't told him yet. I want to make sure. In case anything goes wrong early."

"When do you think it will be?" Aunt Maura was suddenly businesslike, the herb-woman counting up her medicinals.

"December."

She put out her arms and I went into them and was folded up in her familiar smell. I wanted to stay there and feel her arms around me, feel that I had connections and roots and ties, all the things it seemed that I had lost.

"If I can be there for you, I will," she promised. "If I can."

Chapter Twenty-five

———◆———

"I'M AFRAID."

The words came out, just like that, without any more thought than was taken by the cricket as it chirped in the corner of the room.

The rasp of its wings seemed to echo, "I'm afraid," and the hundreds singing in the meadow beyond the shuttered window picked up the sound, a chorus, "I'm afraid, afraid. I'm afraid."

"In general, or in particular," said Arden, his voice raspy as the edge of the cricket's song.

I stared up at the dark ceiling. When I was a child, I used to sleep curled up, on my side, but now another child grew in me, a girl or a boy, curled closely. Now I was most comfortable on my back. Arden lay beside me, also on his back, one hand outside the blankets and the other laid heavy and warm over mine.

"Both," I answered.

He shifted his leg against mine. His skin was warm and very smooth.

"You can't handle all the things there are to be afraid of in one bundle," he said. "Start with the first thing. The others may not be so bad."

"The baby..." I started. It seemed so much my baby, carried inside me, that it was difficult to think of him or her as our baby, together. Selfish, yet the baby—my baby—was living off my blood and my breath.

"Yes?"

"What if something goes wrong? What if it comes early? What if it comes feet-forward, or I'm too small?"

I put my other hand on my stomach and felt my heartbeat, muffled and far away, and felt the movement of that other, like a swell of water, an answer.

"Your aunt will be here..."

"If she can." I moved my hips, trying to ease the ache that had settled permanently in the small of my back.

"She'll be here."

"It's too far to Middletown. Anyway, I'd rather have the baby all by myself than have that old midwife Wood fussing over me. I know her. She bought blue cohosh from us, kept calling it coohoosh, and I doubt that she knew how to use it any more than she could say it."

I pulled my leg away from his. The quiet settled between us, and like an echo I heard the peevishness in my voice.

"It's normal for you to be worried. I would be worried if you weren't. Of course, you have no control over this, and it's difficult—very difficult, to have to wait and not be entirely sure of the outcome."

Gently, I moved my leg back against his.

"It's not just having the baby," I said. I wanted to explain, without fumbling, without getting angry. "From everything that I can tell, I'm having a normal pregnancy. I feel good, really, and I'm strong. It's not having the baby that I'm afraid of, not really. It's more what will come after. Raising a little girl or a boy—things aren't the same as they were for my mother."

For a moment I was blinded by the light of a memory of water, and walking in the park by the water.

"It's never the same," he said. "Not from generation to generation."

"I know, I know. But now is just so much different. Raiders and Harvesters, soldiers. So much death . . ."

He laughed, briefly, in that strange broken sound, and my anger flared.

"I can imagine that a woman would have said the same thing—making allowances for language, of course—during the years of the Black Death in Europe," he said. "Or, say, World War I or World War II. A Muslim woman during the Crusades, a Greek woman during the Peloponnesian War. The War of the Roses, the Spanish Succession, any of the great famines, any of the revolutions or troubled times."

I lay there, barely listening to him, listening instead to the anger brewing like a hard little knotted twin to the child in my stomach.

"Hill country was always the best refuge during troubled times," he continued. "No different now. Mountains are the refuge. 'I lift mine eyes unto the hills, from whence cometh my help.' The Adirondacks are surely full of refugees, and the slopes of the Rockies."

Sometimes he could talk like that, just talk, as though he was up in front of a class. Except now the class was one.

"The Appalachians were never more than an arm's length away from the kind of insular, peasant society they sheltered right into the twentieth century. There was change, but it was change against a background of family and self-sufficiency. When the wars tore the nation apart, this region reverted to settlement economy and settlement ethics—while the cities became hellholes of tribes and war bands, individuals.

"Look at the Harvesters. They're not the same as the cults I saw in the suburbs of Washington. They are the descendants of the hard-shell Baptists and the snake handlers, by way of the television evangelists. The Millenium has come. Perhaps."

I couldn't see much to admire in the ways of the Harvesters, no matter where they drew their roots from.

"The states of NordAmer are in the grip of a great madness." His voice fell, lower, rasping at the edge of silence. "'Who the gods would destroy, they first make mad,' and that is true. We are mad, and bleeding as we are, we continue to wound ourselves. The rumors of war continue, even if they have to be brought on foot, from battles fought on foot."

None of what he said was new. I'd heard it said a different way by Aunt Maura and others.

I'd heard the tales brought by the pack traders at our door then, and I'd heard worse tales told by the scavengers who came to Arden from the wreck of the cities with barter. One would say that the people were rebuilding in a certain city, had a civil government, law. The next, coming a month or two months or a season later, would say he heard from another that the city was burning, was burned, was gone.

It was hard to believe the things some people said, of peace, civilization, in the Southwest or the West. Tales brought so far, over the great empty spaces, and so long in the coming that the truth had likely leaked away. Or maybe they were never true to begin with.

"You know, Neena," I heard him say, "once I helped to deliver a baby."

I turned toward him, the shadow of him. "You did?"

"It was so long ago—I have to admit that I don't remember much but the woman's panting, and the blood. On the carpeted floor of an office. I remember waiting for the ambulance."

"And?"

"The ambulance came and we weren't needed. I never saw the baby born—don't know if it was a boy or a girl."

My memories weighed on me, day and night, though I didn't have the fainting dreams any longer. Arden's memories must have been so much heavier to bear.

"How did you come here?"

"I walked," he answered.

"No, I mean *here*, this place instead of some other place. Instead of Arden-on-the-river."

"A person doesn't always choose where he goes. I walked west, sometimes taking this road or that road. There were places I stopped. Once for a whole summer. There was a farmhouse, with a garden which was gone to seed with volunteer tomatoes and potatoes, multiplier onions, all for the picking."

"Were you alone?"

"Oh, yes. Always." I hurt with the hurt in the three soft, tired words. "And finally I came down this road. Other people came by. It was a good path. It wasn't until a man came a few days later, and offered to barter a bone-handled penknife for a share of the soup I was cooking, that I realized there was something I could do to make myself useful enough not to be bothered. I had walked far enough."

I understood far enough. Eventually a person just hit up against the edge, like water against the land.

"Arden?"

"Um?"

"What do you think—about the baby and all?"

"I think we'll have the baby, and we'll raise it as best we can."

"Is that all?"

"I think the baby's mother is the most beautiful young woman."

"Most beautiful of where? Here? Far Enough?"

"Two weeks' walk past Far Enough."

I lay there, cuddling the warmth of his words around me. His breathing slowed, became even (though noisy, like always, from the Change-damage in his throat).

I was tired, but not ready for sleep. There were so many things to think about.

I wondered what he had looked like before the Change, and if the baby would have green eyes or blue eyes, my face or the shape of Arden's hidden face that I would never recognize.

Then, quite suddenly, I recalled the face of Mary, the Annunciation painting from that old history text. I saw the golden light on her skin and the surprise and laughter in her eyes. And I recognized the greeting in the cup of her lifted hand.

Chapter Twenty-six

DEER HAVE A way of appearing at the edge of a woods. One minute there are only the brown and gray trunks of trees. The next, deer.

Bosker Thomas was wild, like a deer. He walked up on the balls of his feet, lightly, with his head held forward and his brown eyes bright and tense. His thick, black hair and beard were shaggy, like an animal's winter coat. He wore buckskins and furs instead of wool and cotton; he fastened his clothing together with buttons sawed from bone and antler.

Bosker Thomas was medium height but heavy-muscled. He held himself like a buck deer, antlered and full of the autumn rut. All together, Bosker Thomas made me nervous.

He had appeared at the door of the cabin right at the end of the light, wanting to barter. He carried the roughly tanned hides of four deer, and a hide pouch full of horn and antler buttons. They were finer than the ones on his jacket. I supposed it was Colleen's hands that had smoothed the sawed rounds and bored holes in them.

Arden unbarred the door and he came in, his long stride seemingly not interrupted by the wait at the door. He threw the skins across the table and tossed the pouch on top of the heap.

"It appears you have something for me," Arden said, his voice even, his bartering voice, which expressed neither desire nor distaste.

"A person's got to go to the groundhog's hole, not t'other way around." He smiled, but I saw his eyes go flick, flick, around the room.

"A bit late in the day." Arden picked up one of the skins, bent it back sharply. He pulled it from the pile and turned it over, his knotted hands moving rapidly over the surface, feeling where the flensing knife had cut too deeply or where meat had been left to dry onto the hide. The room filled up with the sharp odor of salt and oak bark and animal.

I was only half-roused from my warm drowsiness by his intrusion. I stayed back in the shadow at the edge of the lantern's circle of light, content in the room's warmth and the companionship of my baby, not wanting to be noticed.

But Bosker's eyes noticed everything.

"Fillin' out," he said, staring at the roundness of my stomach, and then, with a crooked smile, directly into my eyes. " 'Tis no time to be having a child, winter coming on. You watch the deer, the squirrels. They breed for the springtime."

Arden glanced at me, and his look said, "Be patient, he'll soon be gone." Bosker Thomas had a reputation for being brutal with women, as well as attractive, as Colleen had learned.

I pushed my hair away from my face and curled closer within the chair, away from the light.

His eyes followed me. After a moment, he turned back to watch Arden.

"Been good hunting," he said shortly.

"It seems so," Arden answered.

Bosker shifted on his feet. He seemed nervous, though I couldn't imagine he was afraid (like most people would be) of the long walk home in the dark. The woods were as much his home as that tiny house with its windows boarded up.

"I see a lot, hunting."

"I imagine."

"Seen a white squirrel, past High Rock."

"Albino."

"Yeah." His dark eyes flicked, flicked, at the corners of the room. "Other things, stranger'n that."

"Yes?"

"Shot a deer. Big doe. I was following blood sign. Tooken me up on the ridge above Penitence, an' I seen something there ..."

His roaming glance had settled on the wall of books, and he stared at the books, looking baffled. His eyes moved across the shelves, but not like someone reading titles.

"In Penitence, it's likely you'd see something strange," Arden said, a final kind of statement.

"You ever been there? Not in the place, just near to it?"

"I've seen it."

"You ever seen what they do there?"

"I've heard."

"Well, I seen it." He licked his lips, and that, too, was half like human nervousness and half like an animal, tasting or sensing. "A man walked into Penitence."

His glance flicked over me.

"I came to tell you. It was the girl's kin—that Ted."

"Are you sure?" Arden dropped the skins and faced him, his hands half-clenched at his sides.

My breath stopped. I put my hand on my stomach.

"Don't make mistakes like that. I know what I seen. Tall, yella hair tied back, beard the color of her hair. I was on that ridge, and I seen him come walking up to the gate—the gate they set in that big log wall?—and he banged his fist on that gate and they let 'im in."

I stood in the half-dark, frozen there, wanting to hear and not wanting to hear.

"Them people just come a-swarming, out of the buildings, all round him. Next thing, I hear this singing, they're all a-singing, that big mob of 'em all gathered around him. Then one man, he stood up on this platform and he starts to talking. Him up there and Ted down on the ground, standing by himself, an' the people all circled around."

"Thomas, I don't think it's necessary to go on."

"You never heard the like of this," he said. "The man was preaching, and the people were answering back, just low, like a moan."

"Enough," Arden said.

"No." I stepped forward, one step, into the dusky outer circle of light. "Let him say what he's going to. I need to know."

The light jumped and settled, like the shuddering that passed over my skin.

Bosker Thomas lifted his head back and looked down his long nose at me.

"It went on like that, quite a bit," he said. "Then they started moving, the whole crowd, and him in the middle. Back to the pond."

The Harvesters did their baptizing in a pond in their village, I knew that. Winter and summer. And now was close to winter—that very morning I'd kicked a skim of ice from a puddle near the door.

"They took a fit of moaning again, some kinda song, I'd guess. All this time, the man not saying a thing. They got around him and moved him down to the edge of the water, and then the preacher and two other men took him down into the water and they held him under, three times."

Arden's face, that to most people showed no more emotion than a stone, to me showed the distant reflection of all the pain and sometimes joy he had. Now his face showed me sadness, and his shadowed eyes were bright with fear.

"The third time he came up, he yelled, 'Forgive!' and the preacher raised up his arms and yelled back, 'You are saved, saved among the last comers, even the last are welcomed at the shining gate of the Lord.' The two men that were behind him, one of 'em grabbed Ted around the shoulders and held him, and the other one, he pulled his head back and he killed him with a knife. Cutten his throat."

I heard Arden breathe out, as though he had been hit, but all I could see was Bosker Thomas standing there, calm, like his voice was in the telling. His eyes held mine, and I realized that he was waiting for me to break and run, the way a wild dog waits for the rabbit to break cover.

I lifted my face up, letting the light fall on me. My eyes burned with the tears I wouldn't let come.

Bosker Thomas nodded, and he turned toward Arden.

I moved back, from half-light to half-darkness, and then past the curtain into the darkness of the bedroom. I struggled with the trapdoor and went down, heavily, into the warm closing-in of the cellar.

I will not cry, I told myself as I felt my way

through the trapdoor and down, down, into the quiet and the private earth.

A mouse rustled in a corner. I found an upended crate, and I sat down. My eyes tried to follow the dim twists of light that floated inside my head, inside my eyelids.

I didn't need Bosker Thomas to fill in the details. I knew the color of blood, coming fresh from a wound. I could see in my own mind Ted's long blond hair dripping water, and his head pulled back, and the shine of the knife. The pictures came and went, and among them were other pictures, Uncle Ted sitting beside me in the herb room, reading, and Ted standing like a giant in the corn, and him arguing with Aunt Maura.

I knew I loved him, once. I knew that I hurt him. But I never knew that I hated him, too, really hated, until I sat there in the dark. Suddenly I felt unbalanced. It was as if I had been carrying many heavy loads and then one was taken away, and the absence of the weight was painful.

The baby moved inside me. It was like someone looking on, or in, at my grief.

I stroked my stomach and it kicked against my bladder, spiteful.

My hand brushed against something on the crate and it rustled. I pulled my hand away, but there was no sound of tiny feet skittering away. I felt toward the rustling thing until my fingers touched it. A dead leaf.

I picked it up. My fingers were my eyes. I saw the crinkled web of leaf-tissue, dead and brown, and the stiff net of veins reaching from stem to the brittle leaf-points.

I cried.

The tears burned on my face, and they burned when they fell onto my hands and arms. Among all the pictures in my mind, the last of them always pond water and blood, was the sight of myself crying and red-eyed. In the dark it didn't matter, where Bosker Thomas couldn't see and laugh at the weakness. Where Arden couldn't see.

I smoothed the leaf in my hand and felt the edges break. It was crisp and cool like paper. I bunched it in my hand and was glad to hear the cracking and breaking.

The trapdoor lifted overhead, sending a long slant of light down the stairs. Arden followed.

I turned away and put my face into my hands.

I heard him come up behind me. His hand touched my shoulder, softly, and then rested there. For the longest time, there was just his hand resting on my shoulder.

"Neena," he said at last. "Neena, I won't say I'm sorry for his death."

I rubbed away the tears and felt a new hotness on my skin. Of course, I thought, you had all the right to hate him.

"Ted's life was shattered before he ever came here. He didn't come out of the wreck of the cities whole, even if he seemed to come out unharmed. He was looking for a—solution, a way out."

"Getting killed?"

"It's a solution others have chosen."

"But why? Was it because of me?"

"Neena, it started long before you."

"But it ended with me. He might not have done that if it hadn't been for me."

"No." He took hold of my shoulders with both hands. "Never think that. Your uncle was hurt, inside, hurt when he came here. It was like a wound festering, until finally it has to heal or it kills. Maybe he did both. Ted wasn't dragged into Penitence, like others. He went there, knowing what was there. Neena, he wanted forgiveness and he wanted death."

"He didn't have to die like an animal. Like a calf. Like a pig."

"No, he didn't. But sometimes things come full circle."

"What do you mean?"

"Nothing."

He let go of my shoulders, moved across the strip of light, and pulled another crate back beside mine and sat down.

"It's not nothing. Tell me."

"It was a long time ago. Ted killed the man who tried to steal from your place. I think you know it happened. You don't need to hear about it."

"I'm not a child!" I exploded at the tone of his voice, so sure, so knowing. "Look at me! I'm carrying a child—your child. I'm a woman. I can't wait for you to decide when I should learn things! What am I supposed to think about Ted when there's so much I don't know?"

He started slowly. He told me how he came to see Ted chasing the man through the meadows.

He told me how he found them, the man pitched forward in the hay, dead, and Ted standing over the body with the knife in his hand. I shivered at the telling, though he told the story plainly, because it filled in the gaps in what I knew or had guessed.

"He killed the man out of fear, not anger," he said. "Ted was a fearful and unhappy man. That was why he tried to bend others to his will. As I said, his life was damaged; all the blood that's been around him is flowing from a wound you couldn't see."

We all have wounds, I wanted to say, but it sounded hard and cold in my mind and not at all the way I meant it, that Uncle Ted had no right to hurt others just because he was hurt. Not when we all could say the same.

"Arden?"

"Um?"

"Do you really think he's dead?"

"Yes."

He must have realized that his voice said more than that one word. I remembered the fear I'd seen in his eyes, earlier. Then, I'd thought that fear was for me.

"Why were you afraid?"

"Afraid?"

"When Bosker Thomas was telling."

Arden sighed. "I was afraid of what I'd feel when he was through telling. Or, really, what I wouldn't feel. I was afraid, my Neena, that I wouldn't have any emotion at all to hear that he was dead. And if that was so, then the Change went deeper than my flesh."

"Did you? Feel anything for him?"

"Not one thing, Neena. A half a dozen emotions, together, pain and acceptance and happiness and anger. For a long time, Ted Daucherty was a symbol to me of the war itself, as I know I was for him. But his dying broke the symbol I'd shut him inside. He died twice—as that symbol, and as a person, a human being."

"Do you really feel sad?"

His hand touched my arm, moved down to my wrist. He took my hand and lifted it to his face. On the smoothness of his skin, unseen there in the dark, I felt tears.

Chapter Twenty-seven

———◆———

NOW THE WIND howled at the corners of the log cabin, threatening with the cold of the whole length of winter. Now it was good to sit near to the fire and work, and wait for November to pass.

Even more, it was good to sit by the fire with company, a woman's company, as I felt the baby forming toward birth. I looked up from my work, mending a torn sleeve on Arden's oldest shirt. Aunt Maura raised her eyes to meet mine.

Her patient brown eyes, steady against the coming winter.

Just a week ago it had been fall. Then the skies were brilliant blue above the last brown and red leaves. The air was cold, but the sun was still warm. That was the day Aunt Maura came.

I hadn't realized how important it was that she be there, not until I saw Heidi and Sunny come plodding along the road. I was standing at the bedroom window, looking toward the sun. The cart appeared, the rich autumn light blossoming all around the dark form that was Aunt Maura. She was bent over the lines as she drove; she was swaying with the lurch of the wheels into the ruts.

I realized that while I was marking the fall of the leaves and the shortening of the days, it was her I'd been waiting for, watching for, all the while. I had swelled with questions, been marked with the blue veins of questions that wanted her answers.

I ran to the front door and opened it, but I stood there with my hand on the latch and waited.

She whoa'ed the oxen right beside the door, got down, and tethered them to the closest pine. Lawyer came out of some hiding place by the barn, walking stiff-legged until he caught Aunt Maura's recalled familiar scent.

"You're here," I said.

"Yes." She pulled on the worn sleeves of her coat. "I said I would be."

I didn't remind her that there was never a

promise, just a hope. "I'll be there if I can," she'd said. Between the hope and the reality was Ted's death, and that was something we couldn't talk of, not yet. The shadow was too close.

"Let me help you." I reached for one of the bundles on the seat.

"Daneen!" she scolded. "You're carrying enough weight around already without any of this."

I reddened, reminded of how little time had passed since I had been in her house, and a child.

"She's right," said Arden, behind me. He'd come up quiet as a cat, the way he could sometimes.

I threw up my hands and stepped out of the way. Arden and Aunt Maura faced each other across the brown grass.

"I should say welcome to our house," he said, his voice huskier than normal.

"Thank you. We've known each other a good, long time, Arden."

"But we've not been neighbors."

"Not really."

Aunt Maura was strong, but she wasn't what you'd call a really big woman. The wind took the loose ends of her hair and lifted it in fine, soft wisps. I might almost have said she looked frail opposite Arden, but there was the kind of respect that showed between them which would never allow for weakness.

"Come in," Arden said.

They began to unload the cart. There really

wasn't much—Aunt Maura must have just closed up the house and left things. The bags of herbs disappeared down the cellar hole, and her clothes were in a single bundle.

The bed of the cart was full of fodder. Arden unwrapped the lines and began to lead the oxen away.

"Wait!" Aunt Maura came running from the house. She steadied herself with a hand on the rusted metal of the bed, and reached under the seat. She pulled out a package wrapped in wrinkled brown paper. "Okay," she said.

The cart rolled away, Lawyer following and sniffing at the tires.

"Daneen?"

"Yes?"

"This is for you."

She held out the bundle. I was almost afraid to take it—she held the package as if it was delicate, as if it would break to pieces in her grip. I took it with both hands, but it was soft, yielding.

I pulled away the paper, and the flowered lavender dress, Ditsky's gift, spilled out.

The paper fell to the grass and tumbled away. The fine material of the dress caught every breath of wind and puffed with the air. I shook it out, and the lavender flowed like cool water over my hands, down like a waterfall on the wind.

"You'll have to wait to wear it," she said gently.

That moment was as fresh and crisp in my mind as a mint leaf. I didn't have to remember

—everything was there like a vision, the picture of her, Aunt Maura, her steady eyes, her mouth, creased at the corners in the beginning of a smile which waited to form, waited for me. It was a dividing moment, when the time-before and the time-after split apart.

Now, a week later. The wind had risen and blown away the golden fall, leaving the brown-leaf and the dead-stick time before winter.

We were drawn in like worms in their co-coons. The fire roared in the chimney, fighting the wind outside. Sleet pellets hit against the shutters.

I pulled the last stitch up firm, then pulled the thread through a couple of times, catching the free loop to lock in the new stitching.

"That was a big rip in that sleeve."

"Mm." I bent my face close to the shirt and bit the thread in two. "He caught it on a piece of jagged metal."

"Let me see."

I shook out the shirt and handed it to her.

She held the sleeve out so that the line of stitching showed in the light.

"There's a frayed place on the cuff—did you see it?"

"Yes."

"This you've done is nice work, Neena. Your stitching's even, and you don't pucker up the fabric the way you used to."

"Thank you."

The half-smile moved across her face like a stray bit of light through leaves. She laid the shirt across her arm and smoothed out the creases, running her hand down the straight bars of the faded blue plaid.

"It takes a lot of cloth to make a shirt this size," she said.

"I found that out when I took apart one of his old shirts for a pattern."

"And cloth being hard to find."

"Yes." I thought about the handwoven wool and cotton cloth that had replaced the old cloth. Some of it was heavy, some light, some well-woven and some so poorly put together that it stretched and twisted in your hands. And nearly all of it was dull-colored, browns and greens and yellows, dyed with the roots and barks we traded by the bundle and the mordants we measured out on a battered scale. A real, bright red, seen in an old garment, a clear blue—or lavender—just made you catch your breath.

She turned the shirt, looked at the other sleeve, the tails. "Not the first time you've mended this."

"No."

"That's something that just goes on, the mending. Never a day goes by that you don't find a rip in something, or something worn through."

Her eyes held mine.

"You've got to keep ahead, got to mend the little rips before they turn into big ones and the whole thing's gone to rags."

"You're right."

She nodded. She reached the shirt across to me. We sat the length of our arms apart, but it wasn't any longer a distance that kept us apart but one that pulled us together, a comfortable space.

"I've missed you," I said, not afraid that my voice trembled.

"Neena—you know how it's been. And I've missed you."

No one stood between us any longer. Not Ted, not even the memories of my mother. We were like two people who for a long time knew each other just a little bit, and now we were close together, learning about each other all over again.

Aunt Maura looked at me for the longest time, her eyes just the least bit shiny with tears that she would never admit.

She took up her needle and began to sew, a steady sound of the needle clicking against thimble.

"Don't forget that frayed place," she said.

Chapter Twenty-eight

———◆———

LAWYER LIFTED HIS great, grizzled head and stared at the door.

"Arden?" I said.

"I'll see."

Aunt Maura turned away from the stove,

where she was stirring a pot of soup, to watch the dog.

Lawyer lifted himself to his feet and walked slowly to the door. The fur stood up in a ruff across his shoulders, making the threat that would have been a growl if he'd had a voice.

It was dark, the early dark of late fall that brings bone-chilling cold when the sun goes down. The moon had risen. It added no warmth; it seemed to take the last color and life from the bare, gray earth.

Arden stepped to the window and, leaning back, peered out through the gap between shutter and wall. After a moment, he moved to the other window and did the same.

"I can't see anyone."

We waited. The spoon struck the sides of the pot as Aunt Maura stirred. Lawyer remained at the door, motionless.

A shiver ran over me, a night-cold brush of fear. As if in response, the baby swooped inside me, a leaping like my heart.

I stared at Arden's pistol, oiled and loaded and ready on the shelf by the door. And Lawyer. They had seemed reassuring, enough to protect me, nearly a year ago. Now the baby curled inside my body demanded more, demanded walls as thick as a fortress, a dozen dogs, a wall of weapons.

Lawyer turned his head and stared at Arden.

Finally, we heard what had alerted the dog. It was a thudding sound, like the sound of a distant ax falling on a tree, but less regular. It was on the road.

Arden looked again.

"The trees are in the way, I can't see. No—there. A single man, with a walking stick. I can see his shadow. He's waiting."

Arden picked up the pistol, silently unbarred the door.

"Be careful."

He left me with a slow, tight smile that seemed to add up all the times he had been careful before.

Aunt Maura barred the door after him.

There was no sound. We listened until the silence began to ring in our ears. Then, it seemed as loud as a shot, was the sound of someone hailing the barterman.

I pushed myself up out of the chair, and went and stood with my back against the wall, so that I could see out of the space behind the shutter. I saw two shadows, Arden's bulky and threatening beside that slim other. The shadows moved, disappeared into the grove-darkness. Moonlight where it sifted through the branches gave tantalizing, brief glimpses—Arden's shoulder, then the end of a long, dark tail of hair.

"Aunt Maura," I started to say, but I was not sure.

"What?"

I shook my head.

It was Arden at the door. She unbarred it at his knock. The house light spilled out into the cold, shining on Arden and on the visitor.

"Ditsky!" she said.

"I thought it was you," I said, half-breathless.

"Princess," he answered, smiling at me and

his black eyes smiling, too, at the same time his long arm hugged Aunt Maura around the shoulders.

He was the same; Ditsky was always the same. There were new patches on his old clothes, the blue-stone earring in one ear now matched by a red-enameled earring in the other. His hair was held back with a twist of undyed wool. When he shucked off his pack onto the floor, there was a new Army-green cloth pocket on the side.

He collapsed into a straight chair, his legs and arms hanging loosely. A person would think he was completely relaxed, except that his eyes watched the steaming of the kettle on the stove with a hungry man's purpose.

"What brings you by so late in the year?" asked Arden, taking the chair across the table.

"Yes. 'Tis not like you to be heading south when the snow's ahead of you," Aunt Maura added.

"Ah," he said, and it was as though he physically settled into the telling of the tale. "Two accidents set me back. Then, to tell the pure truth, I thought my misfortune was tripled when I found your house without cattle in the barn nor smoke in the chimney."

"Accidents?" I said.

"First, my own. I tried a shortcut in wet weather, one I'd used before, but on a hillside a stone rolled loose under my feet and I slid halfway to Middletown before I fetched up against a tree. The tree was what broke my leg."

"Ditsky," said Aunt Maura, with that tone of voice.

"Now, don't be scolding, Maura. I had good reason to be taking the short way that turned into the long way. At any rate, I leaned on my stick the rest of the short-way-around, until I reached Jemison's house. He set my leg and splinted it up good, and I spent the next six weeks eating his food and helping out as I could by peeling apples and plucking chickens."

He laughed. "And that's another tale, those chickens."

"So what was the second accident?" I pressed.

"Jemison himself. He took sick a week before he said I was to have my leg back. I took off the sticks then and there, and it was another month of nursing him that held me in the north."

"What was the sickness?" asked Aunt Maura.

Ditsky shrugged. "The lungs. He couldn't breathe, he coughed, he ran a vicious fever."

"Pneumonia," said Aunt Maura, nodding her head.

"Most likely. I dosed him with teas, the most of which he didn't like, and fed him soups. He raved a bit in the worst of the fever, but he pulled through. And speaking of soups . . ."

She sipped a bit of soup from the bowl of the spoon. "It could use another few minutes."

"You're a true perfectionist, Maura," Arden said. "A few minutes more or less will not make the difference to a hungry man who's walked past the sunset."

"Okay, okay." Aunt Maura laughed as she exchanged the spoon for a long-handled ladle and began to fill the bowls. Her face was flushed with the heat of the stove, and her eyes shone with the happiness of being useful to others.

I got up and waddled to the table, very conscious of my bigness under the blue cotton shift I wore for comfort and the worn coat of Arden's that I put over it for warmth.

We ate, savoring the goodness of food on a cold night. Food is always better in winter, or at least it seems so, the warmth in your mouth and the taste, when the outside is huddled up with snow. I ate as much as Arden, without any shame, knowing the baby lived from the fat of my flesh. Ditsky outdid us both.

He leaned forward as he ate. I watched him as his lips met the spoon. Something different...

"It's gone." The cord that held the red good-luck charm. "Your little bag, from the Indian woman."

Ditsky set his spoon back in the bowl, reluctantly. "Yes, it's gone. You know how it kept my troubles from me. It wasn't till the medicine bag was gone that they caught up with me. A long time's worth, I think, and some maybe not my own."

"What happened?"

"A dispute with the gate guard at Homestead about the meaning of private property. He thought perhaps I should make a donation, for the privilege of leaving, and I disagreed. I'll pay for entry, but not for the going-out. We had a bit of a scuffle—my stick against his wardstaff—and in the process the cord was broken and the bag got stepped on."

"So what was inside?"

"Dangerous things." He smiled crookedly at me. "The breastbone from a bird—that was the forked-stick thing—and another little bone from a rat or a mouse. Some leaves all gone to powder. The rest of it was too ground in the mud to tell. Maybe the power was gone out of it anyway, or I'd not have had the fight with the gate guard, who was the size of the barterman."

"If he had my reputation, too, then surely he'd have made a powder out of you." There was a shadow of sadness at the edge of Arden's joke, but no bitterness.

"I owe my life to my being smaller—and quicker. A bigger man would've gotten in the way of that staff a time too often."

He took up his spoon again.

We exchanged news across the table. I thought of news being like salt, carefully given hand to hand in friendship and hospitality, the weight of the dish and the salt important in the hand.

For the first time, I felt a part of the exchange. I wasn't sitting at the edge, listening to Aunt Maura and Ditsky as they considered the progress of the world. I had my own stories to tell, mine alone. They rested like foam above the deep malt-brew of the stories that weren't for telling, and they were flavored by what was hidden.

Ditsky soaked up the stories. He peddled his news for an evening's meal as often as he bartered the contents of his pack. The stories gathered details as he went from house to house.

Every person had another thing to say. The stories grew, sometimes year to year, becoming almost like legends of long ago, worn shiny by the retelling.

He knew most of what had happened to Ted. It was not much different from what Bosker Thomas had told. It made us quiet to hear again; Aunt Maura turned pale and stared at her hands. Whatever had happened before his walk to Penitence, she likely knew. That history remained private, dark and deep.

Dinner had long been over. The remains of the soup were congealed and gray in the hollows of the dishes. Arden cleared away (insisting that we join Ditsky by the fire) and set out a bowl for Lawyer. We sat, stilled by the ghost of the last tale, trying to warm ourselves at the fire, with the familiar sounds of the dog lapping, china bowls ringing as they were piled together, and wood crackling in the stove.

Arden joined us. We looked from face to face.

"A lot of changes since the spring, Ditsky," said Aunt Maura.

"A many, indeed," Ditsky said, and then, to me, "You've grown."

We laughed, thinking that he meant the baby, but he lifted his hand.

"No, no. Not that. My princess has become a lady. A most lovely lady."

I felt my face reddening, and I looked away.

"When I came by Maura's in the spring and heard that you were with the barterman, I thought to myself, perhaps for the good, and perhaps 'twas not. She's a child, I thought to myself. But the summer's proved me wrong. You're a lady, Daneen Daucherty."

He glanced at Arden, as though that might not have been the proper thing to say.

"That's right, friend Ditsky. Daneen is her own person. She doesn't wear any name as a collar —there's no name I'd give her but her own."

Ditsky put his hand on mine. "I'm happy for you. I'll be looking forward to seeing this child grow into a person as fine as you all are."

"Next you'll be saying you'll cut your walking stick down to a door peg and be settling here," said Aunt Maura.

He held up his hands in a show of fright. "Not that, Maura. But it may be that I'll shorten my route a little, to stop here the more."

I smiled to myself.

Arden got up, opened the stove door, and poked up the fire. He threw in a cherry log as big around as my thigh. The smell of cut cherry drifted out on a back-puff of smoke.

"Of course, I'm no kin ..."

"How can you say that!" I protested. "You're as much family to me as—almost as much as— Aunt Maura. You brought me over the mountains. You covered me with your own coat. Not kin. What a thing to say!"

"Then I'd like, as family, to offer a name for the baby."

"What's that?"

"Rainelle. It's the name of a place that used to be, down in the tall mountains, down in the forests. A pretty name, I thought at the time."

"For a boy or a girl?"

"I suppose it might do for either, but I was thinking of a girl. And I think your baby will be a girl."

"A new princess?" I asked.

"Oh, there will never be a *new* one, Neena. Another princess."

Chapter Twenty-nine

AUNT MAURA HAD wanted to do the things that needed to be done, but now that the night was drawing close I felt comforted by seeing the room clean and proper all around, readied earlier in the day by my own hands.

My baby—our baby—would look first on the gleam of polished wood and the dull gold of the book titles on the wall, books which I'd wiped clean and straightened. The work had kept my thoughts from lingering on the early contractions, irregular as they were, and from worrying about the labor to come.

I sat by the fire, counting heartbeats, my own and the shadowy rapid flutter of the baby's, which I could sense beyond counting.

A contraction came, drawing across my stomach like a band pulled tight. I eased back into the comfortable roundness of the chair.

"Neena?"

Arden sat uneasily forward on a straight chair, watching me, his eyes brooding in the shadow of his ridged brow.

I smiled for him.

"I'm fine." The contraction eased. Everything went forward as it was supposed to. The book on pregnancy and babies, something that Arden had sought from every scavenger and throughout the valley, said that this was the "early first stage." I took comfort in the predictability of the birthing as I did in the warming of my feet by the stove.

"Time I checked," he said, and taking his coat from the peg by the door, he went quickly through the door so that only a brief draft of December air came through. I shrank away from the chill, then eased as the heat washed back over me.

"He's suffering worse than you," Aunt Maura said, her sentence cut short as she lifted the mended shirt to bite off the thread.

"He seemed happy that we're having the baby."

"Until the birthing. That's when a man can't pretend to be an equal partner. That baby's yours—has been yours—until it's born."

I considered that. My thoughts gathered slowly, paced to the slow cresting of the birth process. For a week it had been gathering, the sharp, sudden pains of the baby's kick, low in my stomach, the show of blood, the contractions that came upon me suddenly like a night-terror.

My thigh ached, again. I shifted a bit in the chair.

"Do you think I'll be a good mother?"

"You'll learn."

"What about Arden?"

She looked up. "He'll learn, too. Did you think there was some special kind of teaching for that?"

I shrugged. "I hope he's a good father. I hadn't thought about that, at first, but lately I've been thinking about it more and more."

Aunt Maura's steady gaze seemed to go right through me. "There were things about him that made you trust him."

"Yes . . ."

"The things that made me trust him first, and made you trust him—that's a good start on a father."

It seemed like ages ago that I'd first trusted him, leaping out of my fear like a doe over a fence. First to trust Arden, as I shivered in the January cold, and then to like and finally to love him. What had gone into that—that great leap into trust? Things Aunt Maura had said about him, the visit he'd made to warn us, then his own honesty and admitted hurt, everything coming together on that night so that I could break free from the snare of tangled fear and love and memory that had held me, no more able to move than a rabbit.

"A father isn't the same as a mother."

"No."

I had a memory, or what seemed to be a memory, of my own father's face. Westin. He was my father, but not the same as other children's fathers who lived with their mothers. It had been just me and Mom, together, and that had been good. Even so, I imagined that a lot of things might have been different with a father.

A contraction came swelling up through my pelvis and my stomach. It was sooner than I'd expected, and stronger. I put my hands on my stomach, and it felt hard. I was familiar with the muscles in my arms and legs and back, the way they'd knot up for work and then hurt after being strained, but this was different. My stomach clenched like a fist. I wondered how the baby could stand such pressure.

Finally the contraction eased, but it was followed a couple of minutes later by another.

Arden came in. I saw the candle flame flicker.

Aunt Maura kept sewing, but I saw her eyes on me as often as on the work in her hands.

I counted through the contraction. A minute. Then I counted. Two minutes and a half, nearly, and another contraction came and my body knotted.

Late first stage, I repeated to myself, trying to see in my mind the charts and diagrams on the water-stained pages. Late first stage, late first stage, until the clenching released.

"I think I'd like to go to bed now."

They helped me to the bed, the little bed I had slept on at first, low and close to the fire, but now bolstered up with pillows and with sacks stuffed with goose grass and sweet grass and mint.

Arden's hands were still cold.

I took a chill from his cold hands, shivered, limp for the time between the contractions. Aunt Maura covered me with two quilts. One had a pattern like a huge repeated flower, a sunflower.

The contractions came steadily.

Arden knelt on one side of me, Aunt Maura on the other. I pushed myself deeper into the pillows, feeling that, wrapped and guarded, I would last through the worst.

Another contraction. They seemed hardly to have any space between. My breath came out hot and sharp between my teeth.

The contractions came regular as heartbeats or breaths.

Suddenly, there was a gush of warm fluid between my legs. The bed was soaked.

"Your water's broken," said Aunt Maura. Steady. She always was steady.

There was a brine smell in the room, a soaked wool smell, and wet skin smell. I couldn't believe that much fluid had come from me.

The birthing rolled over me like a storm. Quicker and stronger, contractions gathering like thunder. Pain like lightning. I was a ridgetop, an oak tree. I was struck, and split apart, and the tension in my stomach rippled and stormed. Pain.

Pain.

I heard myself, like some other person, panting with the pain. Like the cow, gone down, panting. Huh huh huh.

Lightning struck, and I arched to meet it.

I beat with my hands against the wooden rails of the little bed.

Arms went around me and something blocked the rays of light.

"Neena," Arden said. "Neena, I'm here."

His arms folded me around. I lifted up my arms to his neck, but their strength seemed gone and I fell back, rocked in his embrace, in his warm familiar smell.

"Concentrate," he said. The rest was just a murmuring, just a hum.

I saw through the gap between his arm and his body a particular sliver of light. I focused on it. I refused to let my mind and my eyes wander away. The contractions rose up in me and crested and faded. I stared at the sliver of light until my eyes burned like the wick of the candle.

The rhythm came back: contraction, ease, contraction.

I closed my eyes and lay back. Arden gently pulled his arms from beneath me, but kept one hand on mine.

The birthing terror that seemed ready to carry me off was gone. I could breathe. The contractions could be counted. There was time, again. The storm went away, like a summer thunderstorm that threatens and then moves north or south, away.

My body was hot and limp. The contractions pulled it together like a thread taking in cloth. The blood smell hung in the still air.

It was so quiet that I could hear my own

breath, and Aunt Maura's and Arden's, the three threads in a braid.

We all seemed to hear it together, for the first time. It was a steady drone overhead. An airplane.

I felt Arden's hand on mine. It wasn't a squeeze, just a sort of pressure.

He started to get up.

"I'll go," said Aunt Maura.

I heard her stockinged feet shush across the floor, then the shuffle of boots. The door opened and closed behind her.

The drone of the motor in the winter air reverberated in the quiet house. I didn't have to look at Arden, didn't want to see the same ghosts that were in my eyes staring back at me. I returned the pressure of his hand.

When the motor noise changed, one of us started.

It was the longest passage. The airplane moved across the sky slower than an ox-cart rutting up the road.

The door opened.

"It was heading north," she said. There wasn't any need to ask. "The markings—NordAmer. They were NordAmer markings. Bright and clear, the moon showed them when it turned." Her voice was full of wonder.

A contraction came, and I went back into myself, more concerned with the knotting in my stomach than the strangeness of an old airplane flying somewhere.

Chapter Thirty

———◆———

I WANTED TO PUSH. I pushed.

There was a knife pain down in my pelvis, down where the baby was being forced through my flesh.

There weren't contractions anymore. Just steady clenching.

It was a hot-knife pain. A blade heated on a hearth, blackened in flame, twisting inside me.

I pushed, and grunted. Pig-grunted, calf-grunted, bloody and sweaty and shaking with cold.

Someone pressed a cool cloth against my forehead. It smelled of rose petals and green herbs.

Water dripped down my face and ran down my neck.

Push. Push.

Before the wars, the constant forever wars, there were hospitals with white walls. There were nurses and doctors. Women had their babies easily, helped on every side, and there were soft white beds where they lay back and held their perfect babies.

The water formed runnels down the back of my neck. It was cold as ice water. I shivered.

Push.

I was cold. The drifts of snow were piled higher than my little bed, higher than the walls of the room. I sank into soft white snow, chilled, but the hot knife in my stomach burned through me and melted the snow into ice water, a pool of ice water that lapped over me.

The baby came bobbing up through the water. It was sleepy-eyed, like my doll Tiny Sarah, in as pink dress trimmed with lace that sagged and floated.

It was stiff and wide-eyed, little curls pasted against the sides of its fat face.

It had blue eyes like Uncle Ted.

I swam after it, and it sank through the clear ice water. I dived after it, but the coldness took hold of me and lifted me back to float on the surface. Under a white sky. Under a sky where an airplane circled, circled.

The water smelled of roses and trampled grass.

"Neena."

The voice came out of the sky. I closed my eyes against it.

"Neena, I'm here."

Arms lifted me out of the ice water.

"Neena." Arden and Aunt Maura, calling.

I opened my eyes.

"Arden. I'm so cold."

He lifted the blankets up over my shoulders and pressed against me, his own warmth coming through the blankets.

His own warmth.

Aunt Maura draped another blanket over the both of us.

The snow was gone. I rested in the between-time, not cold nor hot now, the contractions faded away like the dreams. I was too tired to worry. I wondered what hour of the night it was.

"Would you like something to drink?" he whispered, close under the tented blanket. "Something to eat?"

"No," I whispered back, my throat raw.

"Water?"

"A little."

I sat up enough to sip the water, and my throat eased.

"I was having horrible dreams," I said.

I drank a little, and then, because Arden urged it and his face was so set with worry, I took a couple of spoonfuls of applesauce, which was tart and strange in my mouth, tasting of dried apples. It made me want to vomit. I pushed the bowl away.

My body gathered itself.

"Oh! Oh, now!"

I could feel the baby coming. Push, push, push. Down, and out.

My stomach felt big enough to birth a whole family, and heavy with pressure.

"Aunt Maura!"

She lifted up the blankets, off my bent legs which hung apart, useless.

"There's a little blood," she said.

I could smell the blood. I could taste it with my skin.

I pushed.

The panic was gone. The dreaming was gone. I pushed, making my baby be born, making it live.

"I can see the head!"

Push, push, push.

Arden held my hand, tightly. I locked my fingers around his and used that solid point like a lever, to push against.

"It's coming," Aunt Maura said. I felt her hands between my thighs. Then a small, wet body, passing from my body into her hands.

"Oh!" she said. "Oh!"

I struggled to see past the blankets.

"Is it all right?"

Arden squeezed my hand so hard I thought the bones would break. "Our baby. A girl," he said.

A girl. Like Ditsky had said.

Aunt Maura lifted the baby up, above the blankets, the cord dangling, and she held her by her feet and slapped her bottom.

A strong cry.

"Let me have her."

Arden pushed back the blankets and Aunt Maura laid her, red and damp and wrinkled, on my stomach. Then she took two clean pieces of lacing and tied off the pulsing, blue and pink umbilical cord, and cut between the knots.

I held out my arms. Aunt Maura lifted my baby to me.

She breathed, another breath to twine with ours, a soft, steady breath.

I stroked her face, a perfect oval, the delicate bird-wing cheekbones, high and fine. Dark hair, damp against her head, which was pointed slightly from the pressure of the birthing.

"Rainelle," I said to her. She fisted up her little flower-hands.

Arden knelt there, waiting. His face was damp. He was crying, silently.

"Our baby," I said.

He nodded.

Rainelle rooted against me. I held her with one hand and unbuttoned my long shirt with the other. I laid her against my breast.

She licked at my nipple, her damp mouth pressed against the heat of my milk-filled breast. I brought her closer, breathed in the sweet blood-aroma of my own.

Arden seemed to waken, slowly, like a dreamer. He lifted one thick hand and brought it, trembling, against us, stroking Rainelle's skin and my breast. I shivered with the fullness of that touch.

I looked up at him. His face was soft as when he slept, the muscles slackened from their normal set. He didn't smile; he seemed at perfect peace. I tried to trace behind his alterations the original flesh of this father, father of our wonderful, perfect, beautiful child.

It didn't matter. I saw what I wanted.

Aunt Maura lifted the softest blanket over us, to protect us from the cold. She folded back the edge from Rainelle's head. She stroked her fine hair, following the soft cleft of her back.

"She's our baby," I said, gasping as Rainelle rooted against me and, opening her mouth, took the nipple. "All of ours. Yours, too, Aunt Maura."

She rocked back on her heels, faintly smiling. "We're all family, aren't we?"

"That's right," Arden said.

Aunt Maura smiled wider, then she turned back to her work, cleaning and washing. I felt her touch, and it was as if she communicated something to me, and me to Rainelle, and Rainelle out to us all.

"Her toes," Arden said. His hand still rested against us, against Rainelle and myself. Gently, he reached down to touch one pink foot, then he lifted the blanket higher, to cover her.

I lay there, tingling from head to foot, aware as I'd never been before of my own skin, once taut and now flaccid on my brown-lined stomach, stinging and stretched in my vagina. Over my breasts, it was thin as a single cell, thin as water, hardly a barrier between me and Rainelle, between my own self and my new, newly-parted-from self.

I turned my head toward the window.

"It's daylight!"

Arden stood up and went to the window. He opened the shutters, pressed his hand against the frost to melt it, and looked out.

"A gray morning," he said.

"Morning," I repeated. The whole night had passed in the birthing, and I'd not had a clock to count the hours, or stars to tell them by. Rainelle had started her passage on one day and finished it on the next, small journeyer.

The gray light sifted through the glass like snow. I turned back to Rainelle.

She tipped back her head. Her eyes opened.

I looked down into eyes as deep a blue as an October sky. I might have fallen in, as into still water, or pulled myself up to circle with hawks.

"Arden?"

"She's waiting for us."

She blinked and looked, unfocused, at us both.

"What?"

"Our future," he said. "Rainelle's waiting for us."

About the Author

As an award-winning poet, Valerie Nieman Colander is no stranger to the literary scene. Now her science fiction tales have earned her recognition in that genre. Valerie lives in the house she and her husband built in the hills of West Virginia. She is the 1988 winner of the PEN Syndicated Fiction Series.

A Message To Our Readers . . .

As a person who reads books, you have access to countless possibilities for information and delight.

The world at your fingertips.

Millions of kids don't.

They don't because they can't read. Or won't. They've never found out how much fun reading can be. Many young people never open a book outside of school, much less finish one.

Think of what they're missing—all the books you loved as a child, all those you've enjoyed and learned from as an adult.

That's why there's RIF. For twenty years, Reading is Fundamental (RIF) has been helping community organizations help kids discover the fun of reading.

RIF's nationwide program of local projects makes it possible for young people to choose books that become theirs to keep. And, RIF activities motivate kids, so that they *want* to read.

To find out how RIF can help in your community or even in your own home, write to:

RIF
Dept. BK-2
Box 23444
Washington, D.C.
20026

Founded in 1966, RIF is a national nonprofit organization with local projects run by volunteers in every state of the union.

THE GUARDSMAN

P. J. BEESE AND TODD CAMERON HAMILTON